THE LAND OF LATER ON

THE LAND OF LATER ON

ANTHONY WELLER

PUBLISHED BY

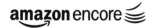

Published by AmazonEncore

P.O. Box 400818

Las Vegas, NV 89140

ISBN-13: 9781612182254

ISBN-10: 1612182259

By Anthony Weller

Novels:
The Garden of the Peacocks
The Polish Lover
The Siege of Salt Cove
The Land of Later On

Travel:
Days and Nights on the Grand Trunk Road: Calcutta to Khyber

History (editor):
First into Nagasaki
Weller's War

for Kylée,

my heaven on earth

The Land of Later On

I   *GETTING MY BEARINGS*

 1   Hello, and Good-bye   p. 3
 2   Arrival   p. 6
 3   A Search for Missing Persons   p. 11
 4   Wayfaring Parents   p. 17
 5   The Root of All Evil   p. 19
 6   A Bed for the Night   p. 22
 7   Old Haunts and Old Friends   p. 25
 8   Immovable Properties   p. 31
 9   Lost Loves   p. 36
10   Who Lucy Was   p. 42
11   Good Manners and Hitler   p. 48
12   Music Everywhere   p. 52
13   Deities   p. 61
14   The World Over   p. 64
15   Hiring a Guide   p. 70

II   *THE JOURNEY*

16   A Café on the Bosphorus   p. 83
17   Why You Might Not Want to Keep Reading   p. 94
18   Lucy's Expedition   p. 99
19   A Serious Misstep   p. 105
20   A Break   p. 115
21   Through the Himalayas   p. 122
22   The Great Game and Its Master   p. 130
23   A More Serious Misstep   p. 140

24 In the Marquesas   p. 144
25 Your Friend, Walt Whitman   p. 152
26 Finding Lucy   p. 159
27 Lessons Learned   p. 170

III SEND-OFF

28 The Return   p. 181
29 Embracing the Inevitable   p. 191
30 Famous Last Words   p. 196

I   Getting My Bearings   1

II   The Journey   81

III   Send-Off   179

I

GETTING MY BEARINGS

HELLO, AND GOOD-BYE

I don't expect to be believed; I certainly don't expect to be understood. Of all the voyages of discovery that men have survived, mine is the most distant, the most accidentally courageous, and also the most far-fetched. So I'm not counting on a medal. Still, if you ever commit suicide on a hot July afternoon in Manhattan, the question of an afterlife is bound to come up. Even if you carry zero hope of tracking down a woman who died four years earlier, on the same day.

One truism of a travelogue is we never question whether the author's actually been someplace. In the old days you could invent a journey to Patagonia, complete with men whose heads grew below their shoulders, and if you had a talent for tall stories the public was none the wiser. Then one day the guidebooks sprang up like buttercups, and everywhere was ruined.

The Land of Later On, as its residents call it, is far from ruined, and you're headed there whether you believe it or not, since you're going to die. Don't worry, that's the good news; the best news is I plan to arrive ahead of you. It wasn't my choice, only my rotten luck and heartbreak, that I was yanked back. And as soon as I'm done writing, I'm going to light out for that territory once again.

The *why* isn't complicated. Though I'm young—forty-eight—my body is far from young, racked by one of those neurological diseases that always happen to someone else and which are such a challenge to people's politeness when they pass you on the street. Relatively speaking, it isn't "suffering" to limp jerkily along with a cane or rolling walker but otherwise look undisfigured. However, in the last few years my right hand had given up its ability to play the piano, which was my profession. The Lucy I shared my life with, whose love and contrary humor kept me going, had died. I'd lost all determination to stick around, much less drag myself across the pavement without falling. My body had unraveled; I had every reason to think this would get steadily worse until I was forced to give up my tiny walk-up and enter a charitable assisted living facility. The other scenario, according to my statistics-minded doctor, was that my disease, which sneered at drugs, would devour me horrifically. Either way, while it was still in my power to decide, I wanted out.

Plus I now had virtually no money left, and that nothing was worth half what it was a year before. I'm sure you know what I mean—the fact that many of us were in the same leaky boat didn't prevent the waters from rising.

As a longtime bassist of mine used to say whenever we finished: "This gig is history, ladies and gentlemen, and the fabulous flying fingers have moved on."

Shortly after I arrived in the afterlife I was offered a guidebook to the place, covered in red leatherette, as if the musty edition contained all I'd ever need. With plenty of sensible advice that turned out not to be true. Everyone, I soon realized, is handed the same malarkey. (Lucy's term, by the way; prescient as usual.)

For reasons I'll explain later, when I returned here against my will—kicking, gasping, alive again and able to remember it all—I managed to carry the insidious thing back. I've written this to tell what happened to me, and make it clear what humanity is up against. The worst fate would be for you, when the moment comes for your own copy, to swallow its cunning words as gospel.

Think of me as Robinson Crusoe in reverse. His problem, shipwrecked on a small island, was to let the world know he was still alive. Mine, rescued from an immeasurable island, is to describe how I was dead till recently. And happier for it.

Happiness, of course, lies behind every travel manual ever written, implying that if you go somewhere, you'll wind up content. *I'm here to warn you that the guidebook you'll be given should not be trusted.* I promise that where you're going will prove more lustrous and diverse than what my mother called the land of the living; yet happiness depends on the decisions you make soon after arrival. Make the wrong choices and you'll find yourself scammed. Hastily reborn, shipwrecked in the wrong place at the wrong time.

Though writing an anti-guidebook was never my idea, my hope is still to save you from cataclysmic errors. If I can't convince you of the destination that awaits you on leaving this life, then I guess it's my fault. But it's your funeral.

I was lucky enough to encounter a stranger who befriended me, and made my search for Lucy possible. Without him, I'd never have grasped the vast conspiracy in the Land of Later On—subtler, more perilous, than any serpentine guidebook.

Many earthbound psychologists would argue that every journey, down deep, is an allegory for the trip we all eventually must take. This idea doesn't begin to provide the strategic help you'll need.

I will. As Lucy said, stay with me.

ARRIVAL

Though travelers seldom stay long, this guidebook will prove indispensable. At entry no passports are required, and customs formalities are lenient, as luggage is never forwarded. In crossing the frontier a small supply of tobacco is allowed. There is no duty on cigars.

Passports? Customs? Luggage? Cigars? Are they kidding?

The problem is that by the time you read this, you're already there and it's too late to pack an overnight bag. Some people find the paradox quaint.

Not surprisingly, travelers are anxious about this stage. *Will it hurt?* Well, no. *Will it take long?* Nope; a swath of infinite blackness, then you're through to the other side in one enormous exhalation. But because everyone's minds are filled with claptrap from those who've had "near-death" experiences, they're expecting a modernist corridor straight out of a cylindrical 1960s spaceship, with blinding lights and welcoming hazy figures.

It's not like this. One moment you're alive—maybe struggling to breathe in a hospital bed, surrounded by impatient relatives; maybe hurrying across the road without looking both ways; maybe one more victim of a freedom fighter's bullets—the next moment you've arrived. There's no corridor, no turnstile, no Checkpoint Eternity. You know exactly what's happened. You're not beset by doubts or jet lag, though the initial remorse can be overwhelming. This feeling dissipates.

And when your subconscious grasps the inevitable, you do relax. You *know*, with every inch of your being, that nothing can be done anymore. We've all seen those nature films of a snake swallowing a field mouse, and watched the mouse—relaxed, accepting—blink out his final glimpse of sunlight as the jaws engorge him. You don't forget that sensation of farewell; you do forget the terror and the teeth.

What does it look like? That depends. Whoever set up the process figured out that the transition would be a lot easier if the scenery were just as you want it. I suppose this means some people find themselves in baggy white togas, trying to balance on baggy white clouds, while others get the streamlined spaceship routine.

For me it was like stepping off a Mediterranean ferry boat from decades ago as it pulled into an intimate port at twilight, the air scented with jasmine, the cafés afizz, the lamps coming on, with a medieval fortress and craggy mountains looming: a heavenly vision I'd imagined but never experienced. *Funny,* I remember thinking, *so this is the afterlife.* I swiftly forgot that minutes earlier I was lying amid sweaty sheets in my apartment, waiting for the pills I'd gobbled to take effect.

Notice what I did not think for even an instant: *Am I dead? Where am I? Who are these people? Can I go back?*

Nor whether I was imagining things, since for the first time in years I was standing upright like a normal human being, having walked off the boat as smoothly as everyone else, without a cane. So where was Lucy? Around me a crowd strolled, enjoying a balmy breeze before dinnertime, and every brown-haired woman seemed to carry hints of Lucy in her energetic walk as she strode past, not recognizing me.

Each one possibly her, but not her.

"What did you expect, Kip?" said a gruff voice. A firm hand tapped me on the shoulder; I turned. In front of me now, on the cobblestones of that serene port, was Dr. McMillan, our family practitioner when I was growing up, the sort of country doctor able to convince you that you'll be fine no matter what ails you. He was standing there improbably in his white coat, stethoscope around his neck, and to the best of my knowledge he'd been dead since I was about twelve.

"What are you doing here?" I asked.

"Same as you. Except I'm not here."

"Are you going to tell me I'm not here either?"

"You're definitely here. I'm only a temporary figment of your imagination. Seems I'm the person you trusted the most unwaveringly during your life."

If I had disputed that, I might've learned something. Still, he had steered me, squalling for dear life, out of my mother.

"So if you're not here, where are you?"

"Oh, I went back. Waited till Genevieve joined me, then we decided, after a suitable while, to try again." He hesitated. "Reincarnate, I mean. This'll make sense once you get your bearings. We enjoyed your jazz discs, by the way. A few items filter through as residue from later eras, if you know where to look. We were very sorry to learn about the progressive multiple sclerosis. You won't be troubled by it now." He chortled. "Talk about a medical opinion you can take to the bank!"

"But where is this, doctor? The last time I saw you—" I was about to utter something not true; for the last time I saw him he was made of wax, the first corpse I ever saw, laid out in a funeral home, hands folded across a blue tie. "—was when I came to shovel snow off your driveway. You met me at the door in your bathrobe and gave me a dollar tip, and told me to be sure to look after my mother. I never expected to run into you at some place that looks like—what, Positano? Portofino?"

"Consider yourself fortunate, young man. An instant after I died I found myself at a sticky Florida golf resort, surrounded by a political convention. I thought I was in hell, until someone explained the law of rising and falling bodies."

"I'm all ears."

What my childhood doctor told me, plus what I came to understand later, was this. The Land of Later On is infinite in space and time. Its denizens are only those who choose to stay. They can occupy any place and era they like, for as long as they like. Beethoven, for example, may be found most days at his house in Vienna circa 1820, but most evenings on 52nd Street, circa 1943— though he sleeps at home and, especially since he can hear again, hates to be disturbed while hard at work. Mozart stuck around a week, long enough to write four symphonies and make sure he was adored by posterity (a few musicologists from the future were lucky to find him), then recycled, choosing to take his chances with the next incarnation. Clearly he should've waited before making such an irreversible decision, but most people don't want to hang around in the afterlife, particularly if they didn't enjoy retirement.

Once you feel at home you can transport yourself to any where or any when you want. You can set up headquarters in your idyllic little Mediterranean port and stroll out across the cob- blestones of, say, 14th century Mecca, or 19th century San Fran- cisco, or the airborne walkways of next century's Singapore. You can have breakfast on one continent in one century and lunch on another in another. For some people this sounds like heaven;

others never go anywhere. Why risk an unpredictable journey when you can stay home, surrounded by loved ones who died before you did, while awaiting those yet to come? Death doesn't bestow a sense of adventure on people who never had one in the first place. A lot can go wrong, grievously wrong, if you don't know what you're doing.

As Shakespeare murmured (no, he's not here anymore either, though he stuck around longer than poor Mozart), there's the rub.

After you remove death from the human equation, my family doctor pointed out, time acquires a different meaning. With eternity stretching before them, people get bored. "I know Genevieve and I did," he said. "Plus there's a snowball effect. If you decide nothing new will happen, that's all you think about. Perhaps not right away, but pretty soon. These sensations creep up. You'll be surprised."

It is difficult to convey just how peculiar you feel trying to tell someone you know is a) not there, b) dead, c) older and wiser, that you don't believe him.

"What about," I asked, "finding the person you lost? Who got here first?"

"It's not that easy," he said, and gripped me by the arm.

A SEARCH FOR MISSING PERSONS

As the Land of Later On contains capaciously every empire, country, province, metropolis and village that has existed or ever will exist, the Editor has chosen to avoid maps of any sort. Nevertheless, he cannot sufficiently caution the traveler. No matter how much this new world may superficially resemble the old, that sensation is misleading and, for most, painful.

There is nothing to prevent you, for the short duration of your stay, from visiting any place or era you wish. But the newcomer is warned that this is difficult to control. And very unsatisfying, for few persons are where we hope to find them.

The reason is mathematical. If we took everyone alive and added all the preceding generations, each crammed continent would spew human beings into the surf like a tram that reaches its seaside terminus. Because the dead outnumber the living many times over, the afterlife has to compensate. Most people, admirably, choose right away to go back to the prior world as someone new.

Long-term residents sneer at this implied housing shortage. "Infinity," as my own guide later put it (shaking his shaggy head by a campfire in a wild valley of the Marquesas Islands), "has room to spare." There's a strong-arm pressure to force you to return, become someone else, start the rigmarole one more time. No matter what they claim, the idea isn't to prevent overcrowding— for the Land of Later On is expandable, like a map you can unfold and unfold for as much terrain as you need—but to keep the finite bloodstream of human personality flowing.

What tormented me was whether Lucy might have succumbed. Suppose I'd missed her? In life she wouldn't fall for a sales pitch or sweet talk, she was too savvy. But in death? How long would she wait? What if, after four years, she was ready to give up here at exactly the same moment as I had back there? Or, with so many candidates to choose from, she'd found someone else?

"You must know," I said to Dr. McMillan. "When do I get to see Lucy?"

It might've been coincidence, but at that moment there was a clatter of pans and a guttural imprecation in some foreign language from inside the café.

"That's always the newcomer's first question," said the doctor genially. "Though not with me, because I knew Genevieve was right where I'd left her, safe in the hands of our four grown children. All I could do was imagine Alzheimer's tightening its grip. Don't think me cruel, but from this perspective you wind up cheering. You want your offspring to be able to get on with their own lives. And realize she'll join you hale and hearty. So the sooner the better."

I saw Lucy newly arrived, brimming with health again. Could she have guessed how despondent I'd become after her death, swallowed whole by my disease? Would she have cheered it? Imagined me on our shared bed—the bed we'd loved in, the bed I'd watched her rapidly deteriorate in, unable to ease her anguish as she had for me—and figured I'd take matters into my own hands, though it took ten frustrating minutes to force open the childproof bottle of suicide? *Hurry up, Kip, we've got a busy eternity ahead of us.* If so, why wasn't she here to greet me?

"You haven't answered my question," I said selfishly.

"You'll have to find out for yourself. It's not as if your Lucy is someone I'd recognize. She isn't one of these young ladies sampling the evening air, is she?"

"Unfortunately not."

"Describe her for me."

Five foot two, eyes of blue, has anybody seen my gal?

When you have to describe the love of your life, you retreat into a stumbling semi-silence. What could I say to make the doctor respond: *Oh, sure, she's just around the corner—I walked right past her on my way to find you!* I lacked the words to convey Lucy precisely. I'd lain on our sheets only a few moments earlier, waiting impatiently for the sleeping pills I'd gulped down with glass after glass of Manhattan tap water to do their job, staring at the favorite picture kept resolutely by my bedside; but it was a large photograph in a frame, not something crumpled in a dying man's hand, so I didn't have it to show him.

Presumably there must be a kind of information kiosk around here where you could make inquiries, where they kept alphabetized dossiers.

"Is there?" I asked.

"Nope," came the dreaded answer. "You're on your own."

The photo belonged to another era—the late 1980s, when a pattern was being laid for outlandish events decades later. Genocide, disease, starvation, a war on the ecosystem; as Lucy put it, "Like watching the planet commit suicide, but no one leaps to the rescue."

How to describe her?

That portrait was taken on our first holiday together. In those days I used to get month-long stints at hotels set on Caribbean beaches, where waves of visitors came as regularly as sucking tides. Out Saturday morning, in Saturday afternoon.

Lucy was not, perhaps, beautiful or even pretty in any public sense, but to me she was lovelier than any Cleopatra. This did not dawn on me till several months in; I guess it's often like this. One reason I was so attached to the picture is that over the years it became a measure of my deepening feelings. At first it was merely a holiday snap, Lucy with turquoise water behind her, leaning against a mottled palm. Her scruff of brown hair more tousled than usual because we'd just swum. She had come down for a week to join me on my gig, and it was early in our affair, our affair that stretched eighteen years. We barely knew each other; the photo held the energy of our discovering our bodies together amid the press of tropical heat and its unexpected fragrances, far from the wintry city where we lived many blocks apart. Her blue eyes alive with the sunlight that lay around us, beyond the umbrella of shade we were basking in after our swim. In the picture you can see the top of her breasts; her neck whose elegance I hadn't appreciated until I saw it set off by the black loop of a bikini tie, knotted beneath her hair; her "ratty little nose" (that's how she spoke of it, but with all the impeccable instincts of a rat, I would argue back); her careful lips, careful not to say anything she'd regret.

"I'd better warn you, I'm not a natural improviser," she told me on that beach. "It wasn't allowed when I was a kid. So I never learned."

"You improvised our meeting. You could've said no."

She smiled. "I thought I did."

That was my Lucy, and the fact I could stroll any Manhattan thoroughfare with her and notice how other men did not notice her made her even more beautiful in my eyes. Not out of possessiveness, but rather a pride that I could see who she really was. A woman to admire, learn from, and infinitely desire, even as my fellow masculine slugs had not the slightest idea who was walking jauntily past.

"There's no way to find people?" I said to the doctor. "Doesn't seem fair."

"Your conception of 'fair' is going to change very soon."

I was in no mood for an argument. "Let's agree the system's inefficient."

"Is it? If the idea is to make folks exasperated, before they get used to not locating people they've been dying to see for years, it's highly efficient."

For some newcomers, I learned later, the arm-twisting was that glycerine guidebook; for others the persuasion was a spiel from snake-oil vendors. In earlier centuries the message came down from holy men or troubadours. Even my own family doctor was not so subtly suggesting I give up.

"Why not make the place horrible? What's wrong with sheer torment?"

He shrugged. "As you'll find out, frustration or boredom or fear of eternity wind up more persuasive than pain. Genevieve and I decided enough was enough."

Well, when you put it like this, I thought, it's extremely frigging efficient. What could be more typical than I kill myself because it's the only option available, thanks to the miracle of modern pharmaceuticals—which otherwise let me down, having abandoned me to my disease and failed to save Lucy—I unexpectedly break through to the other side, and it turns out she's not here to welcome me?

No letter to reassure me. No current address. No trail of breadcrumbs.

Not that I'm blaming you, my darling. Maybe you have your reasons.

"Remember, some people arrive and run smack into their parents. Or find their way homeward—meaning a place that resembles where they just left, right down to the dust balls behind the fridge—and their loved one is waiting patiently. As if they'd stepped round the corner for a quart of milk. You never know, you might get a happy surprise when you go back to your old apartment."

But he looked away, and I was sure he knew she would not be there.

WAYFARING PARENTS

I have no memory of my father. He was a doctor, a GP and colleague of Dr. McMillan. His was one of the first disappearing acts in the American upheavals of the early 1960s—a lot of good it did my mother to know she helped begin a social trend. Years later I learned he'd vanished with a patient, a wealthy divorcée who offered a less snowbound existence than our town in upstate New York. By that time my mother was dead (brain tumor, a perfected version of what neurologically happened to me), and it wasn't easy to locate a father who didn't want to be located. So I didn't bother to try. Likewise, if my father had surfaced in the Land of Later On, I wasn't about to look for him now.

My mother was another story. My good sense and exquisite taste in finding Lucy I ascribe to the privilege of knowing my mother: a small, dark-haired woman, London-born. Emigrated in hopes of starting a ballet school and avoiding miserable winters. She succeeded in the first, at least, and having survived the Blitz, working as a teenager with shell-shocked children, she felt sure that nothing the New World threw at her would compare to the nightly rain of Nazi bombs. Not having met my father yet, she was mistaken. I did my best, as a boy, to make up for him.

"She's here somewhere," Dr. McMillan told me. "At least she used to be. She and Genevieve had a marvelous time, once we convened. It did them both a bounty of good to be able to confirm each other's memories. But we could see your mother was itching to transport herself to another century, a whole slew of them. It would've been selfish to talk her into staying put. Plus it's not as if you can ping-pong all over the world and keep returning to the present without getting confused."

"Do you know where she was headed?" I asked—though my mind was on Lucy. My mother could wait.

"She said she was planning a whole historical tour of ballet in Europe. She knew plenty of great figures might not still be here, or be performing, but that didn't bother her. She wanted to soak in the fragrance of different eras. But good luck locating her. There's one expression you'll hear a lot—*a needle in a timestack.*"

Where to begin looking for my Lucy, who died at forty-three, full of regret that she'd never really gotten to travel much?

"If I had to do it again," she said once, "I wouldn't have played it safe before we met. I'd have tried living on foreign soil, to see if I could flourish. Then moved to the city in time to find you."

"You might not have felt the same way about me, in that case."

"About *us.* No," she added firmly, "I'd have decided even sooner."

THE ROOT OF ALL EVIL

Though residents dispense with money, since its value is meaningless, the newly arrived may find it psychologically difficult to assert that they be given goods or services free. For travelers determined to handle cash there are innumerable currencies floating around. However, the dealers rarely give a generous rate of exchange. Cheating the ignorant, no matter how pointlessly, remains a frequent diversion. This is the least of the proliferating perils that lie in wait.

In other words, now that you're dead, no need to worry about money. But come to think of it, you'd better start worrying about money. Because even here (if you listen to your helpful guidebook) you can never have enough.

I learned the setup from Dr. McMillan, once we chose a wharfside table and ordered wine and grilled sole. I wasn't hungry, but the prospect of a meal with him —I guessed he was going to leave me afterward—was deeply appealing. A funny thing about appetites in the afterlife is that they spring purely from pleasure.

"Here's the challenge," he said. "Eternity turns out to be just one day after another, without any prospect of the pattern changing." His eyes were kind. "As you well know, Kip, somebody with a neurological disease, not life threatening but definitely life ruining, has a better grasp of the infinite than any philosopher. You can arrive eager to look around, ready to wait for your beloved, then be astonished by how quickly you lose interest." As if against his will, he went on. "Better move fast, buster, because she can go back at any moment. Having eternity in your pocket won't do you much good if you don't find her in time."

"So can you tell me where to start? Or is that privileged information?"

"Start wherever you might expect to find her under normal circumstances. Don't be miffed she wasn't here waiting. She had no idea when you might appear."

"You did," I said.

"Only because you summoned me."

"I still find this hard to accept."

"You'd have preferred Lucy."

"No offense."

"None taken. But something got in the way. Assuming she's still here."

Though I never believed in an afterlife, I'd always imagined it as a sunny outdoor café filled with people I wanted to see, and a decent piano in the corner. It never occurred to me that the person who mattered most might not stick around.

I knew where to begin searching, anyway.

The bill came, brought by a mustachioed waiter in a white smock. The doctor examined it gravely, then handed it back with a flourish. "Keep the change."

"Grazie, signore," intoned the waiter, who bustled on to his next table.

"But you didn't give him anything."

"He pretends, I pretend, everybody's happy. For people who want to feel swank, there's plenty of money in circulation. Tourists who want to worry about being broke can always offer to wash dishes. Shall we kill the bottle?"

What I never got used to was seeing newcomers—no matter where or when, swinging Harlem nightclubs or the smoky coffeehouses of Istanbul—fish around their pockets, worrying if they had enough, beset by their own inadequacy. After a lifetime of never having enough, scrabbling to earn my crust as a musician, staying in expensive hotels only if I was playing the lounge, and a final few years watching all Lucy and I had painstakingly saved get siphoned off, it was easy in the Land of Later On to turn my back on money. Thanks to her, I had an idea of what I was worth, no matter how little the world might've chosen to pay me.

A BED FOR THE NIGHT

Though hotels, rest houses, or caravanserais are readily available in all eras, standards have changed. Even with the hygienicizing effects of the after-life, a traveler may find amenities disappointing and sanitary conditions unpleasant. (The bubonic plague no longer exists, yet the 14th century still has fleas galore.) Relief can be taken in the certainty that fears of infection no longer apply.

The freshly arrived usually want to visit home, and will find familiar locales spruced up. This never cushions the fact that loved ones are seldom there. Though the initial panic does pass, the ensuing despair is profound. Most feel an immediate urge to go back to the prior world and begin a new life.

My first night I spent in a room above the café, having said good-bye to my family doctor after dinner. It was there I found the guidebook, two copies waiting in a drawer so I'd feel free to take one. By now a loneliness had sunk in, and a paralyzing fear that I would not locate Lucy in time.

"Don't worry," said Dr. McMillan soothingly. (This instantly made me worry.) "You'll find your way. I suspect that when you go out for a morning walk you'll turn a corner and find yourself on Second Avenue." He allowed himself a little laugh. "In the afterlife, all roads lead to Second Avenue. Then it'll be up to you whether you enter your building. You'll find a familiar key in your pocket, but it'll be your choice if you head up the stairs, fit the key into the lock, turn it."

"I'm ready to go tonight. I may already be too late."

"Take my advice, you need to sleep in first. You've been through plenty."

I had the eerie sensation I'd never see him again, and said so.

"That's true," he answered. We were standing amid passersby promenading around the excited port. There was a festival the next day; boys were handing out candles, and wooden stalls were being put up, hung with banners. "I've done my job, which was to welcome you. You don't believe everything I told you and there's no reason you should. My patients never did, and look what happened to them. Give yourself a chance, you'll learn everything with your own ears and eyes."

I could accept that Dr. McMillan and his beloved Genevieve had returned separately in hopes of trying again, whatever that might mean—though it sounded like a mistake to me. What I couldn't understand was why some organizing force had pulled his name out of my psyche as the person I trusted most, instead of Lucy.

Likewise, I couldn't wrap my thoughts around the notion that if my dead doctor wasn't here, who was standing before me? Was he some kind of projection on a screen? If so, who was doing the projecting? A committee? Me? Then what was to prevent my putting on the sound-and-light show with anybody I wanted?

Perhaps this meant Lucy was gone. Or didn't want to welcome me. Perhaps it wasn't that I didn't sufficiently trust her, but that she no longer trusted me.

What about when I held her in my arms? I thought. When we made love? When she helped me hobble across the street, after my leg went wonky? "Make way for Twinkletoes!" she'd yell to befuddled taxi drivers, one hand on my arm, one holding them at bay, trying to keep up my humor. "Lickety-Split on the loose!"

Don't tell me Lucy, when I find her, is some projection on a screen.

"Nope," said the doctor, though I hadn't uttered a word. "I wouldn't try to tell you that. Think of me as the image left when you stare at something, blink, and look away. Only the living think the afterlife's full of ghosts."

"What about all these people?"

"They're not ghosts any more than you are. As your doctor, I'll vouch that you're healthier right now than you've ever been. You're walking normally, right? You'll also find you can play the piano superbly again."

"I was wondering about that." I flexed my right-hand fingers.

Amid the Mediterranean clamor he waved at what must've once been a storehouse, above where we'd eaten. "If you go up the stairs, you'll find our headwaiter's wife has a room for you. Stay as long as you like—a week, a month. On the other hand, you always had a roaming personality. Just take your time. Expect delays. You'll soon get the hang of shifting. And don't be surprised if you give up and go back. Best decision I ever made."

"I guess now I'm going to shake your hand, right? And it'll feel as alive to me as anyone's hand ever felt. You'll walk away, into the crowd, and when I look again you'll have vanished. But I still won't understand where you've gone."

"Wherever it is the music goes, old friend," he said, and let my hand drop and walked away.

OLD HAUNTS AND OLD FRIENDS

The room was modest—simple wood furniture, a narrow bed, flowers in a hand-painted pitcher. There was a framed watercolor of the harbor, portraying what I saw from the window. The bar below stayed open with the festival, whose hubbub I heard as if through a veil. For once I wasn't troubled by futile dreams: walking easily, or running, most of all playing the piano. When I awakened shortly after dawn, the streets were swept and the makeshift kiosks shut. The port was deserted.

There was a shared bathroom, but no other guests stirring. I took a shower, enjoying my newfound sense of balance and washing off more than the grime of arrival—something like the dead skin of a former life. I used plenty of soap.

When I returned to the little room, a towel wrapped around my midsection, I found fresh clothes waiting, including a dappled green shirt Lucy had bought me years earlier and thrown away behind my back when it fell apart. ("Don't be such a crink. What do you expect? The sword wears out the scabbard.")

Naïvely, gullibly, I slipped that extra guidebook into my jacket pocket. The carnivore slid in perfectly.

Downstairs the café was closed, so I started walking briskly, confident in my auspicious ability to move. If I could walk I could search; if I could search I could succeed. *I knew, Kip, if I hung on here long enough you'd track me down, my darling.* Small fishing boats rode at anchor, their sails furled. The ferry waited in its slip. Above that postcard view loomed the medieval fortress, strands of cloud wreathing one battlement.

Beyond the port I started mounting cobbled lanes that got narrower. I was in a circuitous quarter of shuttered houses. A dog befriended me, otherwise the world was fast asleep. It was impossible not to recall my breakfast routine in Manhattan, when I'd face the ordeal of hobbling downstairs from my walk-up, turn right on 88th Street, and clip-clop with my cane the block down to Second Avenue and a coffee shop where, in that New York way, they called me "chief" for two decades. Near the end, the more unsteady I got, managing a walker instead of a cane, all I could think about was the dilemma of what I'd do after I was in a wheelchair and my stairs became impossible. That was coming as surely as Thanksgiving. Rent control had protected me for a quarter-century; these days I couldn't afford a ten-by-ten storage unit. Move? Move where? The elevator at the Musicians' Union?

I no sooner had this obsolete thought than I came to a branching lane in my Mediterranean port, diverged, and found myself tromping healthily down 88th Street.

Though Dr. McMillan had warned me, I let out a yelp, then caught myself and realized that different rules applied here—in musical terms, like an unforeseen modulation to a remote key which swiftly establishes its own logic. Eventually I was able to accept the transference as normal, to go down a city street in one era and, without having to mouth some magic phrase, find myself a couple of centuries and a hemisphere distant. Some residents never master this trick, but I've always enjoyed the thrill of going instantly from, say, E-flat major to B.

Once I reached Second Avenue, which changed significantly across the twenty-six years I lived half a block away, I could assign it a date: the late 1980s, though this wavered near my coffee shop, the Excellent. *("We may doze, but we never close.")* Shimmering, a junk dealer's tried to become a sushi bar as I passed.

In the Excellent the daily crew was on hand, caffeine vagabonds and others like myself who got up late, having worked late. For years I was the sole musician who frequented the place except for a few months when a country-rock band would stagger in for breakfast as I was leaving; we'd nod with the respect that doomed species grant each other around the water hole. For old times' sake I ordered steak and eggs, as unhealthy and delicious as I remembered, savoring the illusion that I could relive my youth. Of course, this was wrong: none of it *had* happened before, it was happening anew, and we were all dead, every customer, every waiter. (The country-rock band in a plane crash, naturally.) I was not going to meet Lucy and fall in love with her slowly, immensely, on this stage-set of the knowing past.

Abruptly I no longer wanted my scrambled eggs. I nodded to the aged Greek waiter who'd croaked some years back but was thriving this morning. "See you later, chief," he said, and winked.

Standing up, I caught sight of myself in a mirror behind the front booths. Young again, long before thirty, full head of dark hair, direct gaze. Plenty of determination to return to my flat and practice, not imagining that one day my diseased right hand would believe it'd never touched a piano.

I cleared out and strode vigorously up the incline of 88th to my old five-story building. The keys were indeed in my pocket. I let myself into the entryway, whose snot-green walls weren't peeling in the afterlife. Here I'd kept my rolling walker padlocked to a heating pipe, so I never had to wangle it down the flight of stairs. Now, happily, the walker was gone. I didn't bother opening my mailbox to see if I was still receiving bills, went up the metallic stairs quicker than in many a year, found my apartment door. Suppose Lucy were waiting for me?

I knocked loudly. "Lucy, it's me!" No answer. Rapped again.

Behind me I heard three locks snap open with a vicious velocity and the grunt, as if from some primeval animal, when my neighbor pulled his door open. That grunt belonged to Billy Boyd, who'd preceded me by more than a year (stomach cancer, not surprising since he subsisted on coffee and ice cream) and been succeeded in his lease by a dullard nephew. I turned and there he stood, as sturdy as in life, breathing heavily from the effort of confronting another human before lunch: with his billy-goat face and scraggly brown beard, his beady eyes strained from reading Sartre through the cheapest glasses a nearby drugstore could supply, his checked flannel shirt buttoned to the top to guard against unexpected chills, his tan dungarees spattered with a former owner's paint and held up loosely by a belt that was too big.

"Wow, who'd have guessed?" he muttered. "You look *good* in men's clothes."

"Very funny. Glad to see you, too."

"What do you expect, a ticker-tape parade? I thought you'd never show up."

"Now you can go back to bed."

Perhaps Lucy was out for a walk.

"Listen to the comedian. There's plenty to complain about here, believe me, but tops on my list would be I don't require much sleep anymore. I never got up early in my life, and I'm not enjoying it now."

"Hasn't it raised your productivity? I'd expect the masterpieces to flow."

He was the only professional pornographer I ever knew. He treated it as a job, made a living, and didn't take himself too seriously. On the other hand, he got prickly when people were condescending to what he termed the world's second oldest profession, dating to "the first caveman who bragged, with unmistakable gestures, about the beauty he rescued from some woolly mammoth." He was virtually impossible to insult without his topping you, but I never heard him make fun of what anyone did for work. On everything else, it was open season.

"My productivity has nose-dived. Remove the financial impulse, and man doesn't know what to do with his leisure time. You doubtless haven't been around long enough to realize that. She's not here, by the way."

Maybe I had the wrong era. Maybe, as my doctor warned, she'd already gone back and I was too late.

Sorry, I waited as long as I could. But I'm somebody else now, the person you love has been obliterated. What kept you?

"Guess I'll hang around till she appears." He said nothing. "I don't expect being dead to change my determination."

We'd become friends when, soon after he moved in, I wrote him a lilting waltz with deranged harmonies that could've come from some twenty-first-century Charlie Chaplin movie, and called it *Billy Boyd Is a Dandy.*

"No one expects death to change anything. It seems so much like life you forget what life was like. So people decide they might as well just evict themselves."

"Explain something." I needed him to explain a lot. "I do understand where we are, but I don't really grasp *when* we are. I was down at the Excellent—that waiter you autographed a book to was alive, the sushi bar hadn't opened, and Second Avenue looked like 1989. Yet you look, if you'll pardon my pointing it out, a bit older. Clearly you're aware of the last two decades. And your own demise. So what gives?"

"That's the problem with human beings," he snapped. "Always taken in by the scenery. So you happen to be walking around a version of the neighborhood from twenty years ago. So what? Force that idea's tributaries out of your head. There's only one me, bub. I won't age unless I choose to. Our waiter looks elderly only when he likes. He may go home to his wife and they're both thirty again. Rutting like weasels. They may weekend in Renaissance Florence. Right now, as a matter of fact, you're looking as un-laundered by life as when I first met you, and I don't enjoy it one bit. There, that's better. Heh-heh, you don't realize it, but you just aged ten years. The power of positive thinking. Title of the new volume, in case you're wondering, for my *Conrad Cockleberry, Intergalactic Bachelor* series."

"I suppose if I unlock my door, my Steinway will be waiting, but Lucy won't show. Is that what's going on?"

He was impassive. "I can only vouch for this year. But according to the guy in 2A, she's never come round. I wish I could tell you different. I'm glad to see you. I'm sure your piano's in tune. But don't expect miracles your first morning."

IMMOVABLE PROPERTIES

For newcomers, the most emotionally fraught moment is the return to a former home with its furniture and mementos. Sometimes it echoes not the recently departed present but a treasured period decades earlier. The surprise is followed by an overwhelming anguish. Can this really be all I have to show for my life?

"If you don't mind," said Billy Boyd, arching an eyebrow, "I'll sit this one out. Feel free to scratch at my door when you're done screaming."

"Thanks for the encouragement."

"If it makes you feel any better, I was on my hands and knees the first few minutes. But heaven knows I'm a rank sentimentalist."

He had the courtesy, if you can call it that, to slip back into his apartment and slam the heavy door. One, two, three; his locks ratcheted into place with finality.

Better to do it fast, like tearing off a Band-Aid. Keys in hand, an instant later I was in my apartment, staring at the cabinet Lucy and I had stripped of sickly paint—to "the skin beneath the acne," as she called it. We rented a standard New York railroad flat. You walked into the kitchen, congested by a shower stall. To the left was our north wing, with barely space for a double bed and an armoire you had to inch past to the toilet. The armoire was needed because there were no closets; I'd inherited it from Billy's predecessor, who got so fed up with the lousy heat he moved out in a fury. It had two mirrored doors, and Lucy told me shortly after we became lovers that it made her nervous, since it theo-retically showed the works—"some things are better left to the imagination." But the bedroom lay in perpetual darkness because the window opened onto an air shaft which gave us, in stereo, the bickering of an elderly Ukrainian couple versus the heavy metal din of a disturbed loner.

Our luxurious south wing, containing my tiny upright (leased for six bucks a month, about a dime per note since it lacked two octaves), must've been the quietest living room in Manhattan. Past the fire escape it looked out on the token trees behind a long apartment building and, if you closed your eyes, could make you think you were in the country, not a honking city.

I listened carefully for her breathing from our bedroom, as I always had on coming home from a gig. I poked my head in; our ribbed blue comforter was so pristine you'd never guess that two people had died amid its folds. No sign she'd been back—no pile of half-read books on the tiny bedside table. Eternity would not have changed that habit. My favorite photograph of her still right where I'd left it.

Besides my piano, our living room held our tired sofa; Lucy's desk, which became a dining table whenever we entertained; and a squat, chromed armchair in furry brown cotton, acquired from the disenchanted neighbor. Lucy called it the Bear Chair, and we christened it athletically ("We should attach a plaque, Kip,") before we decided its design was too surreal even for us. I wasn't sad to watch it go (we carried it down to the street, it vanished in minutes), but to find it here gave me a pang.

One advantage of such a small flat was that after my balance got weird, if I toppled I could grab a wall or chair or table.

What I felt was far from the guidebook's "overwhelming anguish." My home hadn't changed, but I appreciated it with new eyes. The world exists in all its infinite detail—which, going through the motions, we ignore on a daily basis. Dying, then seeing my apartment in the Land of Later On, made eloquent how much I'd failed to notice. Like the stain on our hardwood floor beneath a living room window, from the palm I lethally over-watered when she left for two weeks to visit college friends in Oregon; now it brought back a flood of poignant recollection that seemed preposterous since I'd been screwing up my suicidal courage in this room only yesterday. And when I sat down at my spinet, as I hadn't for quite a while, I was reminded that this instrument (Lucy cherished its "benign plink") still remembered me as a virtuoso. Is it any wonder the first tune I played was *I'm Getting Sentimental Over You*?

Pure joyous relief to manipulate the piano again, a tactile unburdening so intense it shook my core. What a listener feels aesthetically, a trembling in his soul, a performer feels physically. For an hour I let my fingers do what they hadn't been capable of in years. After Lucy died I stopped practicing with my left hand, having given up on the right, so what was the point? I couldn't gig one-handed. And I couldn't stomach losing the instrument to the point where I played more awkwardly than a beginner. For my loyal students, all of them advanced, my explanations were sufficient.

Beneath the thrill of finding my ability exactly where it had abandoned me, I was reluctant to keep going for fear I might use it up and reluctant to stop for fear it might evaporate. I needed a few days to confirm that one gift of the afterlife was being restored to the pinnacle of whatever I'd had to offer.

What was not on my mind, for a change, was a vindictive migraine of numbers: the number of paces from sofa to desk chair, from chair to kitchen sink, from sink to bed, from bed past that armoire to the toilet. My cane, originally used outside, had become necessary for brief trajectories; on hot afternoons I'd sprawl across the sofa to recover my energy because the bed was ten steps farther. Since reaching the Land of Later On, I hadn't encountered the assault of numbers once.

Indeed, the apartment was a precise, spotless version of the place I'd shared with Lucy. Everything of Lucy was still there except Lucy. When I felt confident enough in my hands to take a break, I went to the chest of drawers next to the Bear Chair and verified her clothes were still in it. I'd held on to a few, despite friends' advice— a pair of jeans, a scratchy red sweater, a white blouse. Despite what Billy said, if her smell were on them, presumably she'd just stepped out for a carton of milk, as Dr. McMillan put it. I held them to my face—no, she hadn't been around. Why wasn't she here? Could she be waiting someplace else where she knew I'd come looking? There'd been an early boyfriend, killed in a motorboat when she was in college—would she have tracked him down?

It was too easy to make lists of grievances, long forgiven in life, which might not be forgiven later on.

I was blessedly interrupted by a pounding on my door which could only be Billy Boyd. I hurried over and let him in, feeling I could outrun a foreign sports car.

"Back in business, I hear," he said. "Not that I'm turning soft, but it's good to have you tinkling away. I suppose you're going to scare up some old gigs?"

The prospect hadn't occurred to me.

"I know what you're thinking, buddy. No need for money now. They might not remember me. Maybe I can't hack four hours a night the way I used to. Don't forget, the chicks love a great piano player."

"Only in your filthy novels. Besides, I'm taken."

"Sez you. Trust me, the afterlife is like the swinging seventies all over again. No killer diseases. No jealousy."

"No thanks."

"Don't dismiss the professionalism of doing something well. There's no pressing need here for dirty books, but I keep scribbling away, my publishers keep putting them out, and people keep asking for my work." He spread his hands like a priest bestowing a benediction. "Look, man needs live jazz like he needs classic pornography. You have to embrace your special standing in society. Besides, it'll give me a reason to go out at night. I can tell the pretty girls I'm your friend."

"Fine, if it'll help you get—"

"There we go. Want to grab a cheeseburger in an hour? Or are you starting to feel a little nauseous as the reality of where you find yourself sinks in?"

"Sorry, I ate." But he was right.

"Don't worry, it passes. You'll have some gnawing questions by dinnertime."

"I'll bang on your door."

LOST LOVES

Along with the frustration that plagues any traveler who expects to find loved ones, only a thimbleful of solace may be found in exploring the past. Memory is not exact, but the afterlife is. Just as returning home after a journey can be unsettling, seeing a place that you believe you recall accurately will dismember that belief. Home—or anywhere you were happy— is always worse than you think it was.

Deviously worded, don't you agree? Get frustrated, give up. But I hadn't yet cracked the guidebook, and I wouldn't have been dissuaded from searching for Lucy.

"To the living," my own guide pointed out once, "the world rarely improves. It takes being dead for a while, exploring the past in all its dung and glory, to grasp that our nostalgia isn't for the scenery that's been lost, but for our youth."

Since Lucy wasn't in the apartment we shared for so long, I'd have to hunt for her elsewhere in our past. I figured I might as well begin at the beginning.

I'd first met her at a bank on 37th and Lexington. For my early years in the city I took any gig that came my way, and the lunchtime circuit wasn't a bad one. Back then banks were inventive about luring customers, and having a pianist play light classical or standards from the Great American Songbook was cheaper than giving away toasters. The pianos tended to be baby grands, the banks didn't care if you subbed out for something better (grocery store opening, Broadway show, office shindig), and there was a steady stream of work. We were paid to practice. The gigs went from eleven until one and paid $50, decent money. You had to wear a tie and alternate Gershwin with, say, a movement of Haydn, followed by *Danny Boy*. You got requests; nice old ladies would cash their Social Security checks then make small talk with the pianist who knew tunes from their youth.

Some musicians feel this kind of gig is beneath them. I never minded. The pianos were better than my spinet, lucrative private parties came my way as a result, and I never found shame in bringing music to people. Occasionally I was able to coax the phone number from a pretty woman stuck in line beside my right hand.

Usually these gigs lasted months, since the agent would slot you in and forget you; unless the bank got a deal on toasters, you might be there forever. At Lucy's branch I was only a sub, but fortunately it was on Fridays, when she made deposits for the flower shop on Lexington where she worked several days a week.

I missed noticing her my first lunchtime   she later swore she noticed *me*—spotted her exuberant walk and straight back my second—traded smiles on her way out my third—vowed to get her number, or at least give her my card, on my fourth Friday, before the regular pianist stopped spending long weekends with a Stamford girlfriend. That summer I was in tiptop shape, running every afternoon around the Central Park Reservoir; my health difficulties were more than a decade away. My playing had turned a corner, and I was starting to believe I might make a mark.

My final Friday I sat behind the keyboard with a card prepared in my jacket pocket, on which I'd scrawled *Willing to travel*. Not the wittiest line you've heard. It referred to the engraved side of my card, which had my name, number, a stylized drawing of a piano, the moneymaking phrase *All Styles* ("Jazz & Classical" confuses people), and the motto *Have Fingers, Will Travel*. By 12:45 I'd abandoned hope. She always looked so fit, so compact—maybe she was at a gym, exercising.

She walked in with ten minutes left. Nodded at me rather coolly. She was more smartly dressed than before, skirt and blouse rather than jeans and T-shirt. She took her sweet time filling out the deposit slip. In honor of her stylishness I switched from Arlen to my most soulful fusillade, the Chopin *Prelude in E minor*. She turned from the teller and started past the piano. I could either amputate the piece and offer her my full attention, or talk above it.

Then she stopped right next to me.

"I used to play the piano," she said. "But I gave it up."

"It's never too late to learn again."

"Malarkey. Everyone has limits."

"There's nothing wrong with making music for the sheer joy of it."

"That's what all piano teachers say. I suppose you give lessons, too."

"I have to survive."

"You still shouldn't mislead the innocent."

This was not going the way I'd planned. She could vanish at any instant. At least Chopin, useless Chopin, was finally over with.

She said, "You do that very well."

"Thank you. What style of music did you play?"

"I didn't get as far as a style."

I said, "Well, I'm finished here." This to set up an offer to walk out with her. Up close, she was not as pretty as from afar, but she had the most luminous blue eyes, more curious about me than I deserved, and they were with me right to the end.

I made as if to shut the keyboard. The bank, sensing danger in their New York way where no threat existed, had installed a padlock that I was expected to fasten. Before I could get up, Lucy slid alongside and all but elbowed me.

"I'll show you what I used to play. The only piece I got anywhere with."

I stood politely; a lesser man would've seized the opportunity to remain seated next to her. I was expecting *Heart and Soul*. Instead I got Chopin's *Minute Waltz*, delivered with full velocity and unhurried phrasing, which I always describe to students as an ability to breathe musically. I was flabbergasted, and said so.

She shook her head, shook those curls. "One swallow does not a summer make. It's fascinating what the body remembers when you stay out of its way."

"You must've played for years."

"So what? Better to leave music to the musicians."

"I was hoping to get your number. Maybe we can have a drink some evening."

"I don't drink." She shut the piano lid, and I was alert enough to reach across her lap and snap the padlock closed. "I'm not looking for piano lessons."

"I understand that."

She said, "I was hoping we could have lunch today."

Unavoidably, when the woman you love dies, you wind up laying your first memory of her alongside your final glimpse. This solves nothing. In the afterlife the pasts keep multiplying, and the person you're searching for is never in any of them.

Yet it made sense now, as it never had in life, to align my recollection of meeting her with the anguish of watching her close her eyes the last time, riddled with leukemia in our apartment bed and not strong enough to hold my gaze; she'd insisted on remaining at home. *When I die, the world dies with me,* she said to me faintly that morning. *And only you will be around to remember any of this beauty.*

She'd have discovered this was wrong four long years ago. Four years to get bored here with waiting, to decide to go back, to unself herself.

Having conferred with Billy—hearing me play again had fired his resolve, he said, and he wanted to focus on his magnum opus, involving aliens—I decided to visit that fortuitous bank. I took the Lexington Avenue subway and successfully willed myself back to what sure looked like August 1987. Beginner's luck. The bank was open, some contented tickler was at the piano (I'd forgotten it was a Mathushek), the tellers looked listless like all tellers in the Land of Later On.

I stood trying to memorize the place, hovering near the piano. I was tempted to tell the guy I'd warmed that bench myself. At that moment, as I glanced through the wall of glass to Lexington, remembering those Friday noons of hoping she'd appear, who should appear across the avenue but Lucy, a Lucy young enough to be from that era in our lives, walking purposefully, ignoring the bank and all it meant.

I dashed outside, thinking: *That wasn't complicated.* The bank entrance was on Thirty-seventh Street, but it only took seconds to get through the door and reach the corner. I looked right, left; from my side of Lexington I had a view up and down the block.

I didn't hesitate, I yelled her name and ran first one way, then another. She could've turned onto 37th or 36th by now. No Lucy anywhere. I sidestepped traffic and stood in the avenue, jumping to see over people on the opposite sidewalk. This disappearance just was not possible. She'd ducked into a store. Or hopped a taxi—there were a couple already dwindling a few blocks downtown.

I couldn't have mistaken her profile. No way.

Honking cars forced me out of the avenue to the other side. I searched along every aisle of a pharmacy, an office supply store, a framer's. In the massive lobbies of several buildings. I crossed back over and stood in front of the bank for a half hour, hoping she might emerge somewhere. A sudden inspiration sent me racing to the flower shop where she worked for nearly a year, back when we met, but they'd never heard of her, and I didn't recognize any staff. So much for the flexibility of time. The bank was still there, like her flower shop, everything looked and sounded like the right year, but Lucy was gone, gone, gone.

No, I told myself, that wasn't entirely true. I'd learned something enormous: she was somewhere in the afterlife. Waiting for me or not, she was still here.

Unless what I'd witnessed was a last glimpse, before she winked out of sight forever and became someone else.

WHO LUCY WAS

I wish I weren't constantly exhausted. Writing this—even dictating it onto my laptop, as I'm forced to—wears me down after a couple of hours. Still, I plan to be done soon enough, and at that point I'm out of here. These clumsy fingers will quit the building again, with no mistakes this time.

Another lesson you learn is who your friends are. They are not, for example, those well-meaning visitors who stare down at you in the hospital bed, shake their heads and cluck earnestly, "You know, you've still got a lot to live for." Because you've just had your stomach pumped (not as pleasant as it sounds), and the nurses won't allow you a pen because you might open a vein, you can't jot down a list of heartfelt reasons for sticking around. Nor, since I was brought up to be polite, do you mount an argument. No, you lie there and take it. Like a psychological enema.

It turns out your friends aren't the ones who stop by to say *Hello, you lovable dope* or *Why did you do it?* or *Welcome back!* but those who realize the regret in your eyes flows from an undertow of failure. And all you're offering is a chance to say good-bye (knowing you're bound to try again) and ask (not that anybody has the nerve) what dying was really like. My musician friends, ex-colleagues who heard about my attempt and came to see me those three days in hospital, knew why I'd tried to check out. Their only surprise, they said, was why I waited so long. Which struck me as strange, since even after Lucy's death, even with my disease, I never thought I came across as suicidal. I guess it's the quiet ones you have to watch.

I don't believe Lucy and I stayed together for any obvious reasons. Oh, I found her lovely from the beginning, though not everyone saw what I saw. Our sexual life never deserted us; balanced, we kept to each other's orbit. It undoubtedly helped that I was away for a week here or a month there.

None of that is what held us together. Nor was it because she'd always been a jazz fan, and loved my playing; nor because we respected each other's minds or enjoyed not agreeing on much. It had more to do with an amused befuddlement at why we fitted so naturally . . . and thus we kept our mysterious experiment going.

After I got ill and lost the use of my right hand, and later some coordination in my left, she tried to get me to write a memoir about learning to play the piano, now that I was no longer able to. "Kip, I know there's a special writer in you," she'd say. "At least for something you know so well. Who better to write it?"

"*How to Be A Successful Racehorse,* by Tomorrow's Dog Food. Right?"

"I wouldn't frame it so optimistically," she said. "But that's the general idea."

Our arguments were not severe. One thing we did agree on was that there was no afterlife. Perhaps this came from not having family. We were contentedly alone, and as we got older any sense of what we'd missed dissipated. There were no holiday feasts to feel imprisoned at, no obligations to anybody but ourselves, no support systems beyond what we provided each other. It hit home when my mother died that I truly would never see her again, and since I had no family to hang around with in life, why should there be any after death? To be a grown-up without children or relatives robs you of all sense of genetic continuity, much less immortality. For Lucy, on her own at sixteen, it was much the same.

Neither of us was religious, either. The only temple I worshiped at was human talent. I must admit that after a drummer I worked with died young, of a skin cancer he neglected, I did ponder resuming our gig at some jazz club in the sky.

All this changed with Lucy. Her death left me dreaming I might see her again—although I couldn't sustain such hopes, since I knew she'd never believed.

"My guess," she'd said, "is you don't even know it's over. As if somebody turned off the lights. You don't realize what happened after the fact, because there is no after the fact. The blinds come down, the door's locked, no one's home."

This was on our second date. Admittedly, there are few places better to debate the afterlife than a neighborhood Chinese restaurant. We ended up going back to my flat, ostensibly to talk, hopefully to fool around, but ten minutes later she was lying on the rug moaning about MSG poisoning while I wondered if this might be her excuse to cab it home. But it only infiltrated her nervous system first because she was smaller. Within minutes I was by her on the rug, matching her moan for moan.

"Maybe this is what it's like," I said. Heroically I kept us supplied with gallons of water, and at last we succeeded in washing away the poison.

"That's your philosophy?" she said, beside me on the sofa now. "You think death is a perfected form of monosodium glutamate?"

"I wouldn't put it that way."

"A sort of streamlined food additive to improve flavor, that turns out fatal?"

She loved to wickedly assault your position, even after you capitulated.

"I don't pretend to have thought this through. There's definitely life after MSG. I don't believe there's immortality. Except if your LPs stay in print."

"No celestial Chinese restaurant. We agree on something."

"I bet we agree on a lot," I said, getting ready to kiss her for the first time.

"Sure you want to bet?" But she let me.

We weren't similar at all. She was a natural planner, she wanted to arrive at the airport so early that they were still attaching the wings to the plane, she liked a schedule for each day even on vacation, she'd figured out a better approach to most things and was usually right. I've made her sound inflexible, but she was a genius at making do. This is why she was such a great yoga teacher: she could instantly glean from a situation what was possible, and enable her students to do their best.

After my disease took hold she remained encouraging and funny no matter how difficult our lives became, and after she got fatally ill, she never gave up hoping until the very end. Then her sadness was mostly for me.

Her habits, so unlike my own, improved me. She earned a solid living in the late '80s and early '90s giving private lessons— she'd visit East Side apartments a few blocks and tax brackets away, and limber the wives. She believed everyone had a right to health; she taught at senior centers as well as at one of the principal ballet companies. The goal of a superb teacher is to become unnecessary, and Lucy kept her students inspired. In those years I didn't pull myself together until noon, after getting to sleep late after a gig, but she persuaded me to instead take a nap before work, that it was absurd to miss the freshness of a morning's practice. "Discipline is remembering what you want," she'd say. Though not an original thought, her tone was always so gentle, yet direct, that she could help you change your life.

To be a jazz musician is like waiting on an obscure South Pacific isle for the copra freighter due months ago, bearing mail and roofing, to appear on the horizon. To be a professional in New York—when gigs are drying up here it means they're even scarcer elsewhere—makes you wonder if the freighter has struck a reef. Until my early thirties I never questioned being a jazz pianist; I grew up without a father to pull me aside and say, *Are you sure you want to try this?* I was never looking to get rich, I simply wanted to earn a living doing what I loved. But though I had a workable career and made recordings I was proud of, I knew we were playing a music that signified everything to us but was increasingly irrelevant to the society.

You didn't have to turn on the radio to have this hammered into you, it was everywhere. Why try to convince people that the static racket they were discussing with utmost seriousness was baby talk? A musician like myself, trained classically but who went into jazz, wasn't rare; many colleagues were equally at home playing chamber music as bebop. We had nothing against wanting to dance—most of us had started in high school bands. It was the amateurism we couldn't abide, a brute force that was killing our livelihood. We were like brontosauruses munching the grass after the asteroids had struck, joking that our species might become extinct in some distant century, even as the ground grew more parched with every season.

I didn't take the asteroids personally, but there's no pension for freelance musicians. My colleagues and I spent half of what we earned on rent and the other half on health insurance once we hit forty. Strange, I seem to have run out of halves.

Lucy, despite working alone, maintained a better attitude. And income.

"Look," she said when I got gloomy one evening—after a club I'd played for years hired a DJ—"we'll both live to see an era when what we do is chic. Every other block in every town will have its yoga studio right next to a jazz bistro. We'll see supermodels on TV doing downward dog to sell cars, while Billie Holiday sings some torch ballad in the background with Charlie Parker and John Coltrane."

"They never recorded together."

"You know exactly what I'm saying. It's going to drive us crazy. We won't derive any satisfaction from knowing that our efforts helped make this possible. We'll be old and gray—"

"You'll never be old and gray, my darling."

"Just you wait. Your generation of musicians reveres those who came before—how many nights have you taken me to hear some wonderful pianist who's seventy, plays like a hurricane, and can't get a recording contract? I guarantee you, two generations from now, someone our age won't even acknowledge that *we* ever existed. Much less have a lifetime of professional wisdom to offer them."

"I'm so glad I asked you to cheer me up. Can we go to bed now?"

"I'm not trying to cheer us up. But if we admit there's a train headed straight for us, we won't be so surprised at the roar. We might even be able to devise a plan."

As it turned out, we couldn't imagine what was coming.

GOOD MANNERS AND HITLER

"Look, buddy, she didn't go back, I promise," Billy Boyd was muttering over the bacon cheeseburger dinner special at our booth in the Excellent coffee shop. "She could have, but I'd bet against it. I'd bet this plate of fries, that's how sure I am. She's not avoiding you, she's not angry, she's still here, I know she is."

"I don't believe you. If she were, she'd be at our apartment. She knows it's the first place I'd look. Something's gone horribly wrong between us."

"O ye of little faith. Think Lucy's going to hang around this dump in hopes you materialize eventually? The world's her oyster."

"But she hasn't shown up at our building. Not even once, you said so yourself. You jumped ahead five, seven, ten years, still no note for me."

"Ever consider she's got better things to do than wait for some piano player? Maybe she's in Venice, flirting with Casanova. Maybe she's at the top of an Egyptian pyramid, taking inventory on a sunset and expecting you to appear with champagne. Maybe she's horizontal on that beach where you guys performed your bestial acts under the coconut palms. I shouldn't have to spell this stuff out."

"Sorry to waste your valuable time."

He sighed. "Anything for a friend. One lesson you learn, it gets crammed down your miserable throat, is this: the afterlife is other people. And if you can't stomach it, you can leave. Open ticket, no reservation required. No questions asked."

"You're certainly sweeter than ever."

"Not everybody is. Take Hitler," he said, stuffing french fries into his maw. "Take Stalin. Pol Pot. Any dictator you like. Try to find them. Go ahead, try."

"Why would I want to find Stalin? I have nothing to say to him."

"Lots of other people do. But they're out of luck, because he lasted an hour—don't miss the relish, pal, the condiments in this joint have gone up a notch—then saw it'd get worse if he stayed put and received visitors. So he chose the runway."

"I don't understand."

"Took off. Went back. Joined the unwashed undead. Reincarnated."

"Sounds hasty."

"Like snapping your fingers. Not hasty at all, once he realized there were millions of former countrymen eager to see him, and it wasn't for a cappuccino. Hitler stuck it out longer, a week, then he bailed, too."

"What could anybody do to them? They were already dead."

Billy speared my onion rings with his fork. "If you were tortured and gassed while knowing your wife and kids were next, and you waited years for Hitler to whack himself while he inflicted his ideas on your cousins, you're not going to be in a forgiving mood. The guidebook doesn't bother to mention that little aspect. After it was obvious this was really the man, there was a line of well-wishers miles long ready to enlighten his sense of agony. Life being as it is, a person seeks revenge."

So dying did nothing to diminish such feelings. Amplified them, in fact.

"You've read the guidebook? I ran across a copy this morning."

"Tell me about it. An extra in a drawer, right? You and everyone else. And if you can't read, which most people couldn't until fairly recently, they get you some other way. Trust me, it takes iron castanets to keep yourself sane around this place."

"I haven't read the thing yet."

"Warn me first, so I can talk you out of any misguided conclusions. There's a whole lot more truth in even my most depraved pirate romp, *The Jolly Roger*."

"I overlooked that classic."

"A standout achievement in my œuvre. You always have to be on your guard here, you can't relax. Or pay attention to some stranger's blather about reincarnation. The urge seems tempting, then shazam! Before you can blink, wishes are horses. Oh, the guidebook's not their only method. Those predators will nail you in your sleep."

Same old paranoid Billy. Little did I know.

"Who are they?"

"Is this the coffee-shop inquisition? Do I look like a goddamned philosopher?"

"Actually, you do. It's a legitimate question."

"And no legitimate answer shall be forthcoming. As with all the other very reasonable questions you have. The DNA of the soul. Who giveth existence, who taketh away. Who put us on earth, much less this other place. Maybe it's all hidden wiring.

Maybe there's an addle-brained committee. Maybe it's some complicated fucking joke. Just keep your mind focused on Lucy."

"Will do."

"It might surprise you," he went on, "that though you're dead and healthy again, physical sensation doesn't get reduced—that's what keeps us pornographers in business. Remember what I was telling you about Hitler? Well, no one got in to see Adolf, and he certainly didn't step outside to greet the people. It didn't take him forever to realize they weren't giving up. And weren't about to accept an apology. It's tough being a dead celebrity. Think Bogart stuck it out? Garbo? No way."

"So Hitler's gone back to do the same thing all over again?"

"I doubt it. He'll end up someone entirely different next time around."

"Suppose not? Suppose he tries again?"

"Look, it takes special circumstances for a personality like that to succeed. He's probably some browbeaten bureaucrat. I wouldn't worry too much about it."

"How can you not worry about it?"

"Easy," said Billy Boyd.

MUSIC EVERYWHERE

Churches, cathedrals, mosques and temples are open at the usual hours, though references to the hereafter have been altered or eliminated. Art museums display canvases and sculptures executed in the Land of Later On; no visitor should fail to see Leonardo's recent landscapes, protected here from the winds of time.

Theaters exhibit the playgoing habits of their era. In 19th century Europe, for example, ladies must sit in the reserved loges, and gentlemen wear their top hats until the curtain rises. An enthusiast attending a Greek amphitheater for Sophocles's vanished tragedies may find the wine offered by vendors rather cloying.

Drive-in cinemas are especially fulfilling when physical exuberance in the dark is combined with period automobiles. Decades earlier, organists and pianists are often drawn to the challenge of creating soundtracks for silent films. A total absence of TV and the Internet will prove, however, the final straw for many addicts.

Music lovers generally enjoy their brief sojourn in the afterlife. Along with the revelation of hearing historic instruments and performers, to any-one who passes through death and accepts the emigration process, music becomes more compelling.

For once, a relative candor in the travel guide. As I've always said, music brings out the best in people. When I read the above soon after moving into my old flat, despite Billy's warnings I temporarily gave the book the benefit of the doubt.

To be able to play piano again made death worth living, but the apartment brought back memories I'd suppressed—watching Lucy cross a border as she grew weaker, trying not to make alarming noises from our bedroom and freak out my students while I gave lessons twenty feet away. Some evenings she couldn't force down food, couldn't stand the "disgusting stench" of lettuce.

Though it was easy to dismiss Billy's notions of where she might be, what he said—divorced from the spectacle of watching him talk and eat at the same time—was, as usual, reasonable. My problem was that what made Lucy special would also make her difficult to find. She'd become who she was through sheer will-power, with no help from mismatched parents who split up when she was nine and whose refusal to assume responsibility for their child sent her off on her own as a teenager.

Given the freedom the afterlife offered, every foreign culture could fascinate her. Since so many residents perpetually move around, where to search? I now grasped why any address directory would be obsolete after mere minutes, and why there was no mail or phone service in any era. She could be anyplace, and when you threw in the limitless centuries, to find her by accident was impossible. At the same time I couldn't just hope she'd eventually fit her key into our lock. She might give up at any moment, go back, turn into someone who'd never heard of me.

I hadn't been here long enough to appreciate that eternity really means an endless wait for a revelation that's bound to occur, but not yet. I thought of the McMillans: the doctor had hung on till his wife joined him, and right when it seemed they'd be content, they decided to return and be separated again. Maybe their grand reunion hadn't been all that grand.

In spite of Billy's assurances, I felt shattered Lucy wasn't pining as I was.

My blindly optimistic idea was to frequent places where she might look for me. After the bacon cheeseburger dinner special, I spent that evening alone in the 1950s, wandering the New York clubs, hearing my personal deities—Tatum, Hines, Wilson, Garner, Monk, early Evans. *They* were content with who they'd been; *they* weren't reneging on eternity. No traces of Lucy, no helpful notes left for me at the bar. I did repeatedly run into Beethoven, bad skin and bulging eyes and ears like satellite dishes. I couldn't summon up the nerve to speak to him, though I kept watching his eyes, glued on Tatum's left hand. Fingers twitching as he listened.

Hearing all these masters, whose playing I knew so well, brought home to me an enlarged sense of the patience that I lacked. Music is the triumph of subjective time over objective time; while we're listening, our interior clock stops and we're on Bach time, Ravel time, Ellington time. But once we're dead, and can appreciate time as an endlessly flowing river we've stepped out of yet can step into wherever we like, *every* moment becomes infinitely subjective. I had a lot to get used to.

I'd reached that jazz era through an intense bout of wishful thinking. Billy refused to accompany me and scoffed at my worries about finding my way back. "If all else fails, reach deep in your trouser pocket, ignore the family jewels, and rub your apartment key like it's a holy relic. Try not to slam your door and wake me."

After hearing Tatum at a raucous after-hours joint, I spent the night in my apartment, in the bed I'd committed suicide on not long before. The mattress less lumpy than I recalled. My hands, newly awakened and missing more than ever the vivacious curves of her body, kept me from sleeping.

On my second morning I launched myself to Paris, hoping to run into Lucy. We'd visited for an expensive week early in our relationship—"I'll be your time machine," she said, designing several walks to show me the city Debussy had known. Perhaps, I thought, she went there regularly, retracing our holiday.

Walking along Third Avenue, I took a deep breath, thought hard about the banks of the Seine and the impressionist composers' use of augmented harmonies. Around me the buildings shimmered obediently. The shadows changed, horse odors emerged, the sidewalk repaved itself. One advantage of Paris is you definitely know you're there: it was lunchtime, judging from people chomping in the cafés.

I was at the epicenter, breathing in the broad boulevard of the Champs-Élysées, with the Arc de Triomphe glistening in sunlight. A poster told me the date—May 29, 1913, this rang a bell—and announced an organ concert of Bach that afternoon at the Cathedral of Nôtre Dame. Then I realized what the date meant, and why my subconscious had carried me here.

Twenty years before my death, Lucy and I had stood at this very spot, beside a metro stop where we emerged then set off on a pilgrimage to the concert hall where Stravinsky's *Rite of Spring* had premiered, at the Théatre des Champs-Élysées.

Among the most peculiar aspects of being alive is to realize that things which mean so much to you are a blank to most everyone else. Tops on my list in Paris—Lucy had been sublime at joining my enthusiasm—was the lavish Art Deco theater where two thousand ticket holders transformed into a riot whose din overwhelmed an orchestra trying their best to play the most difficult score hitherto composed. The audience was confronting a sound like nothing humanity had heard before, and they weren't suffused with glib ideas of how they should react. They knew they were hearing something monstrously new, and hated it.

Despite the name, the concert hall wasn't on the Champs-Élysées but a few blocks away, near where the Rue de Montaigne met the river. As I began to retrace our route from years ago I felt invigorated by the logical glory of it all. I took my time walking along, knowing I had plenty of hours on this spring afternoon in my pocket until I'd meet Lucy at the cataclysm (choreographed awkwardly, everyone agreed, by Nijinsky for the Ballets Russes), when a thirty-year-old Russian genius in spectacles ignited a pagan orchestral explosion. The composer Saint-Saens had stormed out after the opening bars, offended by Stravinsky's use of the bassoon past the "legal" top of its range; Cocteau sat out the storm; Proust tried not to get hit by flying canes and hats. Nijinsky, inaudible over the catcalls, teetered on a chair in the wings, shrieking out the rhythms to dancers in Cubist folk-costumes.

But Lucy and I were at this moment moving inexorably toward the actual premiere. (That Christmas, after Paris, she'd given me a book that reproduced Stravinsky's manuscript.) May 29, 1913: it made perfect poetic sense.

And it was practical and direct, like Lucy. Why bother hanging around our apartment? Why search aimlessly for her across the centuries, buffeted by the guidebook's "winds of time" (swirled down an endless drainpipe, more like it) in hopes of coinciding? The incident outside our bank showed how hopeless it was even if you got lucky. But the first performance of *Le Sacre du Printemps* had only happened once; she knew that all she had to do was show up before the stampede and I'd find her. Then offer her champagne, to celebrate our survival.

I sniffed the Seine air. Twenty years back she'd held my hand; that morning at our hotel we'd made love languorously, crudely, on waking to raw Paris sunlight. The edifice rose before me, in a concrete you'd swear was stone, with deco incisions at the top, and inside, I recalled, an enormous Lalique flowering lamp at the heart of the ceiling. As I came closer I wondered how to kill the next few hours. If I got truly lucky I'd spot her early at a table outside one of these little restaurants. Oddly enough, I didn't notice any posters for the pitched battle tonight.

My French was barbaric; on our visit Lucy had done the talking. Fortunately the ticket seller was a woman in her sixties who spoke good English.

"Good afternoon, madame."

"Good afternoon to you, sir."

"I want to buy a ticket for tonight's performance, please."

"There is no performance tonight. There is a violin concerto next week. By Beethoven. Other works are Paganini and Sarasate."

"I'm sorry, I must have the wrong date." So much for my flawless memory. "Perhaps it's tomorrow. *Le Sacre du Printemps*."

She sighed. "You are the seventh today. I should put up a sign."

"I don't understand."

"This is not the original May 29th. That only happened once. Understand?"

I didn't want to understand. "There's no Stravinsky tonight?"

She said with fatigue, "It will never happen again, and no God in heaven will allow you to experience it. The same way, sir, you will never be able to witness Napoléon's coronation, the trial of Dreyfus, or the Americans' entry into Paris in 1944. You will not spy on a young Brigitte Bardot in the nude. Those events are not still happening in the afterlife. No matter what the calendar tells."

I must've looked crestfallen, because she added, "You are a scholar?"

"Just a music lover. I was hoping to meet a friend here."

"Everyone is always hoping to meet a friend here. But it is always *nev-air.*"

So much for the power of music to unite people across space and time.

I must've walked aimlessly for an hour, not appreciating the vanished city around me. I kept following the river. I had no appetite; I took a bitter *café* and considered punishing myself with a glass of absinthe, though I chickened out. Could you get blind drunk in the afterlife? Probably. Then I found myself facing a cathedral I knew, that Lucy and I had visited several times. To hear its organ faintly from across the years was a kind of homage to our past.

I strolled across that placid square, into Nôtre Dame. The concert had already started, I could hear a swelling fugue, and because everyone rushing in late stopped just beyond the huge doors and crossed themselves, I felt I was coming to a religious experience, not a musical one. As a result I misinterpreted what I saw.

Before me, rising through the stained-glass sky of the cathedral, were bodies swimming effortlessly through the air, their eyes closed, their arms lifted in different attitudes, faces transfixed with joy, mouths gaping to inhale what was around them. Apparently I was the only astonished one, the others seemed to have come expecting instant lift-off. After resisting the urge to drop to my weakened knees, I thought: So this is what religious faith looks like.

Was that true? Did it mean every person above me grew invisible wings merely from walking into a vast church? I couldn't believe this, but I didn't believe what I was seeing either, all those flying, dreaming people. A bearded fellow who shuffled in alongside me, guiding his aged mother by her elbow, nodded politely and rose off the flagstones; it looked as if, despite her age, she was pulling him up. They stayed in a holding pattern for a few measures of Bach, then ascended thirty feet. Spatters of mud dripped from her boots onto my head. I closed my eyes, an unbeliever confronted with uncomfortable evidence, and as I did so the power of Bach penetrated my brain, seeped into my soul, and I too was airborne.

There's a reasonable explanation, there always is.

It has nothing to do with angels, nothing to do with God, nothing to do with some purity that engulfs you once you're dead. It even has nothing to do with Paris. I later saw it at an Oklahoma truck stop with my guide, as people listened to a love song playing on the jukebox; I heard of it happening to Balinese swaying before a gamelan orchestra, the dancers with weights on their ankles to stay grounded.

I wasn't witnessing the effect of religion. I was witnessing *music*. It didn't happen always, or because the music was special; it seemed to depend on a group experience of everybody hearing the same thing. A violinist told me that it never happened with composers you had to meet halfway—with Chopin, or Fauré, or Stravinsky. It worked reliably with Mozart, with Gregorian chant, with the blues. I never saw it in a jazz club, since each listener experienced something different.

But Bach is like a bulldozer, and hearing a massive fugue pour out of one of the greatest organs ever built was overwhelming.

It didn't matter that most of the listeners couldn't identify what he was accomplishing structurally in the complex play of subject, countersubject, answer, within the plural forces of the *stretti*; hearing music in the Land of Later On bears no resemblance whatsoever to the passive listening throughout your lifetime. It's a bit like experiencing music on drugs, except that now you can hear everything you thought you were noticing after the LSD kicked in. Each contrapuntal melody, each harmonic gesture, has the enormous meaning the composer intended. It's as if J. S. Bach is speaking to you personally from inside your brain, inside your spine, inside your soul's imagination.

Naturally, if you let yourself go and give in, gravity will step aside. It's the human experience of sharing music wholly together that gives people an unexpected capacity to rise, to lift themselves without having to will it. When the concert was over and we all floated gently down again, I realized that the organist had strapped himself in with a leather belt.

DEITIES

Surely somebody organized all this, right? Somebody wrote the guidebook?

For obvious reasons people show up expecting instant answers, expecting religious visions, expecting to meet a Very Important New Friend. (Myself, I'd prefer Erroll Garner.) It doesn't cross their minds that they might not experience any more revelations than before. The guidebook, which doesn't miss a trick, exploits the sorrow they suffer by pretending in its concerned, irritating way that such disappointments are, alas, inevitable.

To put it bluntly: there is no God, at least not in the Land of Later On. Once this penetrates, newcomers often bolt; their dismay keeps the numbers ticking over. There are plenty of long-termers to tell them about doing a walkabout across what's commonly called heaven, searching for deities on every mountaintop, behind every bookcase. If I sound cynical, keep in mind I was looking for Lucy, not some divinity.

"Why?" Billy Boyd snarled when I mentioned how sorry I felt for them. "They were smug and snug and happy till they got here. Then they find out they've been wrong their whole lives. *Great,* they tell themselves. Michelangelo was wrong, Blake and

Milton were wrong, all the prophets were wrong, too. *Jesus* was fucking wrong. So it's not my fault. Hell, this might not even *be* Heaven. Maybe it's an elaborate loyalty test. Know what? I'll just go back and try another round, I'll be happy again. *Sayonara!* Then they're gonzo, before you can fit a word in edgewise. Think it ever occurs to these morons it's an *intelligence* test? Not on your life."

Take this as a warning, one religion at a time:

Christians will not find anyone answering to a description of either the father or the son (who, local wisdom has it, completed the turnaround as quickly as Mozart or, come to think of it, several dictators). The mother, too, went back, it seems.

Hindus and other believers in pantheons are less dismayed, because there's usually somebody available who claims to be one of their numerous deities, and the fact of recycling comes as no shock. Siddhartha, in residence, doesn't say much, but encourages his followers to plunge back into the flow, planning optimistically to be translated to loftier incarnations the way Billy and I might agree to meet for lunch.

Muslims tend to wind up disappointed, especially the males. Mohammed is long gone; there's no Allah; the promised virgins were a come-on. The gardens of Paradise are hardly worth sticking around for, so most Muslims return straightaway. Hoping, like everybody else, to attain an afterlife that confirms their system. Which is why, like Buddhists, there are so many back here. They fail to consider that even if they're reborn as Muslims, they'll have no memories of what they learned. So their lifelong round of devotion, and an eventual disgruntlement, starts all over.

None of this bothers Jews very much, since they're not expecting very much.

Personally, I'd be delighted to meet a Deity; I want to hear how someone capable of inflicting so much suffering justifies Himself, in His infinite wisdom.

That He does not *apparently* reside in the Land of Later On doesn't prove a thing. Lots of people aren't in the first place you look, or anywhere you expect them.

THE WORLD OVER

The Land of Later On comprises all periods. As a result of this layering of era upon era, languages and dialects shift confusingly. For the visitor who seeks out Marco Polo's Venice, a fluency in Italian will be of little avail. A theatergoer who ventures to 1602 London for a performance of Hamlet *will find the Elizabethan accent so strong that speeches are not recognizable, much less enjoyable.*

Despite what the guidebook warns, one gift of the afterlife is being able to grasp a foreign tongue, at least basically, without a moment's thought. Say you find yourself in Barcelona, along the pedestrian island of leafy bookstalls and cafés, hunting vainly for someone who might be there, if only because she always spoke of wishing to see Gaudí's architecture. A waiter speaks to you in Catalan. You can either freeze, or move out of the way for your subconscious to do the work.

My Lucy learned languages instinctively, just as I could grasp the harmonic structure of a tune on hearing it the first time. I knew she'd be proud of me for catching up. Inspired by my rescue from my disabled former self—walking in a normal gear without doing the bent-over-while-balancing act with a cane—I soon took it for granted in a new country that I could rudimentarily understand what they were saying, the way you take for granted that you can cross a room. But I didn't have a photo of her to show anybody, and I didn't have the verbal chops in anything besides English to describe her to some waiter. So much for Barcelona.

I did keep flipping through the guidebook, though I didn't admit this to Billy. (I mistakenly put his aversion down to envy, since every writer I've met had a jealous streak unknown to jazz players.) After a week I was expecting nothing; I could play the piano, I could probably learn to tap dance, but I'd stopped imagining I might bump into Lucy on Third Avenue. I was glad I was dead, but how long was I supposed to keep randomly exploring? Billy was of no use, having cleared off for a few days in the country at "an elite Writers' Colony" which I suspected was some group grope.

I tried wandering Casanova's Venice—the sap had gone back, people said, determined to disprove the lies about his reputation—and selected a pair of lady's silk gloves as a gift. It was easy to imagine Lucy interrogating shopkeepers ("So it's a classic Venetian pattern? You're certain it was actually embroidered here?"), but they looked insulted when I asked if they'd seen her. Venice had seen everyone.

At least materialists enjoyed themselves. I ran into one gent who spent his time chasing stamps he'd been unable to afford in life; he could step up to a postal clerk in 1857 Aleppo and acquire rarities he'd only dreamed of. His equivalents were legion: book collectors, art lovers, Ming porcelain fanatics. It was satisfying to hunt down a grimy coin in a remote era and chat with a merchant glad to pass it over.

Yet many, even if they weren't looking for their Lucy, ended up frustrated. You can spend decades obsessed with Houdini, arrive and be told it's possible to meet him, do your best to track him down in New York, London, or Budapest, then learn he threw in the towel and made his final escape a day earlier. Even though every inch of the past exists in the afterlife, the Land of Later On has no past of its own. As soon as Houdini left he was gone once and for all, and nothing would bring him back. At some point the new person he became would end up here, but there'd be nothing to link the two. He might be a woman for this incarnation (the clause that gives Muslims trouble), and he'd definitely have no memory of having been Houdini.

You don't have to be a celebrity hound for this to matter, you could simply be in search of somebody who meant the world to you. Who might be anywhere.

I told myself Lucy was still here. No way her disappearance at Lexington and 37th, practically before my eyes, was her vanishing permanently. No way she'd gotten fed up in the short time since I saw her, and returned. No way she'd erased herself.

Even so, no matter what the guidebook asserted, I saw no disadvantages to being dead, especially compared to the alternative of being alive. My every bodily struggle, the daily wear and tear of negotiating the streets or just getting dressed, was removed. I could dream about my past with Lucy as much as I wanted, but after all I'd been through there was no chance of a lapse, an urge to return to the prior world.

As I've said, coming back was not my idea—I wish I were still as dead as Cleopatra. Now that I'm incarcerated in the land of the living, dictating onto my laptop, each afternoon I lose energy so completely I can barely drag my carcass to the worn sofa. My right hand, once among the most dexterous in Manhattan (able to span twelfths in every key, leap lightning chromatic thirds in a single bound), is again a useless claw; my left has begun closing too. If

I had to type, this book wouldn't be feasible. And after I'm done, while I still have the strength, I'm going to make damned sure my exit doesn't get screwed up this time.

The word residents use for what's at stake if you do naïvely dive back in is not soul, but personality—because the wager you lay down each time isn't who you are, but how you're reborn. You'll return as your essential self, but the parents you get, and your circumstances, have a terrifying effect on how things turn out. No one's uniqueness or talent can override the cards dealt at rebirth; it isn't as if humanity has been enriched with a second Shakespeare, a revamped Verdi, another Buster Keaton. They all chose to go back, clutching their genius like a suitcase, and that decision didn't get them or us anywhere.

Cleopatra, I saw firsthand, wasn't so easily hoodwinked. One of my boyhood fantasies was time travel. I grew up dreaming of Egypt—not the ancient version, and not the present-day trauma (I did two months in the piano bar at the Nile Hilton, the gasoline fumes in the boulevards almost suffocated me), but some blowsy 19th century Cairo out of a romantic painting. For anyone patient enough to learn the game, the afterlife really is heaven, though there are limits to how far back or forward you can roam. It doesn't make sense to encourage dino-travel, or have Neanderthals seizing tango dancers. Much less amateur astronauts constantly floating off.

In a morning's further frustration from not locating Lucy, having paid my respects to three pyramids and one Sphinx half buried in sand—a trip we'd often discussed—I took a horse and buggy back to town, fending off touts all the way, and cast about the souks. You might assume most Cairenes would try somewhere else, but people stay faithful to home no matter how noisy and smelly home was. The eternal, non-real Cairo of 1894 still felt plenty real, crowded, and humid.

Then I saw her, fingering some ornate silks hanging outside a shop: lissome, not particularly lovely in her page-boy, but magnetic even if you didn't recognize her. Robed in white cotton embroidered discreetly in gold, and every inch a queen.

"Who's that?" I asked a young man in a western suit, wearing a pocketwatch, who looked like he might speak English. It had still not sunk in that, with a bit of bravado, I'd have addressed him in workable Arabic.

"That's Cleopatra."

"The real Cleopatra?" I asked.

"The very one."

All the obvious questions subsided as soon as they came up: *How many centuries has she been here?* Obviously the entire time, dummy. *Does she live—meaning reside—in this particular version of Cairo?* Nope, why should she?

"She's kind of short," I said finally.

"They all say that," he answered, and bustled on.

Now, you may tell yourself you would approach her in such a situation, perhaps be witless enough to ask for an autograph. I only wanted to engrave an image onto my memory, in case I never ran into her again. A moment later she bit her lip and stepped into the shop—if anyone could close a deal on Egyptian silks without haggling, it was her—and I watched those royal sandals press into the dust. Her ankles were the last I saw of Cleopatra.

It was only after I walked away that I realized the significance of seeing her. If the real Cleopatra was here, this meant that all those well-meaning people through the ages, sincerely convinced they'd been Cleopatra in a prior existence, were fooling themselves. Billy confirmed this: not one single person who "knew" his or her identity in a former life ever got it right. When you jump into the game again, return to the roulette table and place another wager on your individuality, you forget everything and start afresh. A crazy bet, you say, yet casinos stay full of the bored, the desperate, the over confident, the believers.

Through no fault of my own—nor Lucy's—I'm the exception that proves the rule. Who came back as himself, precisely where he left off, remembering it all.

HIRING A GUIDE

Knowledge and courage are everything, in travel as in life. The more obscure a destination in the Land of Later On, the greater the need for a guide. The most fearless traveler may learn to emerge in any century and locale he desires, but it is always preferable to have someone professional expose the dangers.

My mother brought me up to believe that beauty would save the world. I'd lost that belief as my disease eviscerated any illusion that my music would have a part to play, no matter how small. Helpful friends would pass on the insight that I still had plenty to offer as a teacher; they learned to keep this tidbit to themselves.

Lucy and I had always expected to end up a pile of ashes. We never imagined the Land of Later On. Or that eternity's machinations could persuade all but the most self-sufficient (Beethoven, shoveling down his cheese macaroni) to condemn themselves to extinction without giving the place a try. Such an open-ended life—if this wasn't life, what was?—would sooner or later go stale. In darker moments I could imagine her making an irreversible choice. Or finding my replacement.

Then one night, while practicing, it struck me that she'd been wholly content before we met. So maybe, just maybe, she was in the studio where she'd lived back then. After all, Billy had never seen her at our apartment, not once. She'd beaten him here by three years, could've easily come and gone in the meantime, but still.

Her cramped studio—where we'd first made love one balmy evening soon after our shared Chopin at the bank—was in a beleaguered three-story building on Duane Street in Tribeca, between West Broadway and Greenwich. Surrounded by turn-of-the-century dowagers and older Italianate grandees, Lucy's address was destined for demolition as soon as the residents could be ousted. Someone with money might've restored that derelict former boarding house; it was obvious where the salon and dining room had been, the shared water closet on each floor, the small bedrooms for transients now turned into studios.

We both retained a soft spot for it, and not only because it was where we began as a couple. Anyone who takes New York seriously carries nostalgia for the city he never knew; I liked picturing not just its jazz musicians of yore, but its former paperboys. Lucy loved envisioning a failed Melville riding a newfangled elevated train to work as a customs inspector at the docks, remembering youthful escapades among cannibal isles in the South Seas. It was a slight relief to know you were not the first to feel your strength subsumed by the city's.

Thanks to my Stravinsky fiasco, I now thought I understood time's peculiar nature in the afterlife, which was both a meticulous recreation of the past and a refutation of it, since the Land of Later On exists *only* in an ever-multiplying, ever-renewed present. Even if Lucy had, until an hour ago, been sipping a lemonade at her studio on Duane Street, 1987, you couldn't dart back right before she left and find her. The only version of any given moment in 1987 that existed was the current one; the afterlife devoured all events of its own past with an insatiable hunger.

I got off the subway, emerged aboveground, and started walking.

At least her building was still standing. According to the style of cars around me, I hadn't gone back in time. I told myself that if she weren't there I could try to check across the years in case she'd chosen an earlier version. Her street looked calmer, prosperous, better maintained—the afterlife is reliable that way.

The name on her letterbox, one of twelve, made my heart soar: *L. Crandall.*

Would things be easy, finally? I pressed her bell and, miraculously, seconds later (there was no intercom, but she must know who it was) she buzzed me in.

I bounded up the stairs two at a time. It was invigorating to see the automatic sprucing-up effect of the Land of Later On. The mahogany banisters gleamed, the threadbare carpeting on the staircase was plush, the walls no longer oozed centuries of smelly neglect but were covered in period fleur-de-lis wallpaper. No wonder she'd chosen to live back in Tribeca, a hipper part of the city, in this building with much more charm than ours. Why hadn't I been smart enough to look here first?

On the top landing the tall window—plastered over in Lucy's day so only a faint outline remained—was open to the clatter of the street. With an upper panel in stained glass, no less. Her door was beside it.

I paused, saturated with memories of autumn evenings seated on her fire escape in folding chairs, eavesdropping on life below. Maybe we'd maintain two residences. I could install a baby grand at 88th Street and we'd sleep down here.

I knocked gently, in a *Tea for Two* rhythm Lucy would recognize.

I heard her come to the door. Abruptly I felt as nervous as on our first dates, though almost immediately we'd fallen into a shared relaxed genius that we never lost, despite disagreeing about so much.

"It's me," I said quietly.

The efficient click of her deadbolt; I'd installed that sturdy lock for her, after a month together. The door swung open.

My new definition of eternity is the interminable millisecond when you realize you're not looking at the woman you're expecting to see, but at a skeptical man in his thirties with a large head of close-clipped dark hair shot oddly with premature gray and a flourishing beard tinged with white. He wore an open-necked shirt like an artist's smock that might've been made from sailcloth, and baggy dungarees. He arched his eyebrows. He seemed vaguely familiar, and he had the pensive, open-eyed stare you associate with Civil War daguerreotypes. He looked as fit as a buffalo.

"Who's me?" he said. He grinned. "Indeed, who am I? Who's myself?"

I felt bludgeoned. "You're not the person I was expecting."

"And I was thinking the very same."

Over his hefty shoulder, though, what I saw was Lucy's apartment with all her furniture, including the foldout table. Even the oil painting of her as a little girl. I'd seen both an hour ago in our flat uptown. The temporal paradox was wasted on me: all I could wonder about was what fate might have befallen her.

"Is somebody else living with you?"

He shook his head. "Nobody."

"You're sure?" Not that I was calling him a liar.

"There was a young lady, evidently, for a faithful amount of time, but she was gone when I arrived. The lock was unbolted. That can mean so many things. I found a spare key behind some books, so I assume she still has one. You're searching for her, I take it."

I was thinking everything, at top speed. From the corridor, Lucy's studio appeared intact. She might have left a letter for me, if this fellow hadn't disturbed anything. Or at least a clue. If I even knew *when* she'd gone—

"How long have you been here?"

"Only a couple of years. But I used to live in this room, a very long time ago. For a few contented months."

"How long ago is very long?"

"Before your friend. The summer of '43. It was a boardinghouse then."

"During the war."

"No, twenty years before the war. Eventually I moved out to Camden, but I always had a soft spot for the breezes in this room. Mary's and Brown's Boarding House, in those days." He seemed mildly amused. "I'm speaking of 1843. I turned twenty-four that summer."

He'd meant the Civil War.

"You look older," I said.

"Thirty-six. For a while I toyed with looking like the person I became, but I don't necessarily like being recognized. Or seeing an older me in every mirror. I was thirty-six in 1855, and that year signifies immeasurably to me."

"Because?"

"Oh, I discovered myself that year. And the world discovered me. Won't you come in? I have a conviction you belong in this apartment more than I do. If you'd like me to leave, I'll gladly go somewhere else."

I felt sadness settle on me like a cloak. "Lucy wouldn't want that."

"I'll brew us some coffee." He ushered me in. "Of all the gifts from the future one mustn't take for granted, instant coffee never lets a man down." He strode over to Lucy's small stove, lit it smoothly with a match. There'd been a couple of nights when we left the oven door open to heat her studio; I used that as part of my argument to persuade her, after six months, to move in with me.

And there I was, in a small acrylic frame on her broad desk. Leaning against the same palm as in the larger photo of her I treasured. I picked it up and wondered about the last time she'd been here to hold that picture.

"I recognized you right away," said the fellow conversationally. "You're Kip, right? Your name is on the reverse. With the date."

My name, in her graceful handwriting. I put the photo down.

"What I call the perfect procession of the years," he said.

"It wouldn't be like her to just go back without waiting for me."

He said, "I do hope you're right. People are always more capricious than we expect, life is more capricious here. I waited not for one someone but for two, one of each you might say, and both of them came and went while my back was turned. Another, a rarer case, drank from the waters of Lethe en route and arrived amnesiac, remembering nothing of our adhesiveness no matter how I tried to offer reminders. Was it an unconscious choice? I never decided. Anyhow, I stopped waiting. But I salute the endeavor. And I would encourage you to wait without flinching."

He had a curious way of talking, lighthearted and oracular at the same time, a smile behind his eyes but something else vining behind the smile. He was about my age—my age at this moment—but spoke like an older man. Of course, presumably he hadn't committed suicide in his late forties.

He poured us coffee into black mugs I had bought for Lucy, and we sat down in matching rickety armchairs she'd thrown out when she moved in with me.

"You haven't told me your name," I said.

"Walt. Walt Whitman."

In the ensuing silence I finally said, "I don't believe you."

"Everybody's got to be somewhere."

As if that explained it. "Why here?"

"Your friend's room was my favorite, of my dozen Manhattan and Brooklyn boardinghouses. I've found I much prefer living in the late 20th century, so long as I can leave it. Remember, I've had time to sample the alternatives. Camden, New Jersey, where I own a house, has not aged handsomely. The place is full of my belongings, but I don't like the idea of living in my own museum."

"I still don't believe you."

He shrugged. "Have a gander at Lucy's books. You'll see I autographed one for her. It gives me an enormous amount of pleasure to do this. My goal is to make the signed copies more plentiful than the unsigned ones."

I'd memorized part of one of his poems in school. I said, "All right, then, if I say: *I sing the body electric,* what do you say?"

He sipped his coffee. "I say to you that that athletic phrase, due to my own myopia, came and went in later editions, but was always followed by: *The bodies of men and women engirth me, and I engirth them, they will not let me off nor I them till I go with them and respond to them and love them.*"

I used to run into a guy who called himself Thelonious, learned Monk's solo recordings note for note and could play them adequately, even claimed that he was an illegitimate son despite the fact he was white and the chronology made no sense. Just because this bearded character had memorized a poem didn't prove a thing.

He said, "I see you don't believe me. Why not open my book and see if there's any resemblance to my portrait?"

"Don't mind if I do."

I crossed the compact room to her bookcase and pulled down her paperback of *Leaves of Grass*. It was one of those editions which contain every variation of every line; Lucy loved to compare different versions of the same Whitman poem by reading them energetically aloud. Unlike me she treated her books with respect, used bookmarks, detested anybody who made marginal notes in ink. Her copy of his poetry (if he were indeed WW, not some imposter) now looked rumpled and exhausted. Every other page corner was folded down, which defeats the purpose, and the fat paperback sprouted Post-its in many colors. Whoever he was, if Lucy came back and saw what he'd done to her book, she'd slaughter him.

I flipped through. He'd scribbled on it in ballpoint, the scribblings were crossed out and scribbled over, balloons and arrows of more emendations were everywhere. Despite the chaos, his handwriting was lovely.

He'd signed the title page below the printed signature and author's portrait from the original 1855 edition. No doubts: he was the spitting image of himself.

"Convinced?"

I said, "When I find her, you'd better be prepared with a replacement copy. She'll be delighted to meet you, but she didn't agree with your original revisions."

He said, "Imagine how I feel. I page through it and can't believe how much I got wrong. Every idea I had about death, especially after witnessing the war, seems commonplace. To me it was only waste. Wasted tenacity in a losing battle. The afterlife should be a consoling experience, but there's no consolation in having understood so very little."

"Everybody feels this. Besides, your book was meant to be read by the living."

He shook his head. "Poetry should not age, nor become obsolete. All I ever wanted was one book that would read right for centuries, and vibrate like a living man talking to his friend. As you can see, since arriving here I've spent all my time futilely trying to get it right. I go on and on and on."

I knew a superb classical guitarist who only dared set foot in a recording studio once. He then spent years editing that material; everyone but he knew he would never put it out; he was destined to vanish. From the perspective of the afterlife this didn't matter, but I still thought he was totally out of his mind.

How Walt Whitman chose to spend eternity was his own affair, but I didn't see the point of occupying strangers' rooms in former boardinghouses, filling editions of his masterpiece with scribbled revisions in quest of a faultless final text.

Well, I'd finished the coffee, it'd been good coffee; and it's not every sunny morning you sit down in the former studio of your darling and share a mug of joe with a dead immortal poet, even in the afterlife. I cleared my throat.

"Would you mind," I said, "if I look around? Maybe there's something that'll help me find her. And if she turns up, please tell her I'm waiting at our flat."

"I'll let her know," he said. "Tell me, my friend, was she a pamphleteer?"

"She was a yoga teacher."

"I mean, did she collect pamphlets?"

"She was a strict minimalist. Didn't collect anything."

"You might," he said, "want to look in that left-hand kitchen drawer."

Every home has a bric-a-brac drawer; in a New York apartment it tends to be a museum of city life, containing keys that work on cold days, outmoded subway tokens you neglected to trade in, adapter plugs you might need. Lucy was ruthless about stuff like this. It went in the trash, and woe betide the partner who suggested otherwise. My memory of the drawer here was that, like ours, it contained only her grandmother's floral napkins, with cash for the week hidden among them.

I crossed the room to the kitchen cabinet. There were the cloth napkins, and twelve bucks the poet hadn't touched. Beneath was a pile of travel pamphlets.

I glanced through them. Constantinople; Simla, India; Buenos Aires; the mighty Mississippi; Pagan, Burma—there must've been fifty. The array was dizzying. None were from the present, but all were pristine, as if she'd pulled them off a rack in some otherworldly travel agency, since as far as I know they weren't printing tourist brochures back in 1450. In the Land of Later On, somebody was.

I unfolded one for the Marquesas Islands, in the South Pacific. Its typeface looked mid 19th century. The illustrations were steel engravings from antique books—tattooed loinclothed warriors with ornate battle-clubs, mollusk-brassiered maidens in lascivious dances, whalers under full sail on the horizon. It read:

See . . . idyllic tropical isles where Herman Melville jumped ship!
See . . . lush valleys where a young writer lived among cannibals!
See . . . how the heartsick sailor found his nakedest desire!

"I've never seen anything like this. How did she get these?"

"It's not easy. But it can be done." He appeared to be making up his mind about me. "Yes, it can be done."

"Do you know where she might've found them?"

Walt Whitman smiled. "I know a guy, who knows a guy..."

"You've got to be kidding."

He looked as if he might blow a bubble. He leaned forward. "I'm going to tell you a secret," he said, "and you can choose to believe me or not. For many years here I have been a member of an underground organization dedicated to persuading people not to hastily quit the afterlife until they've seen as much of it as possible. Though few in number, our success rate is not negligible."

"So these are your organization's brochures?"

"They were produced by contacts of mine. As I'm sure you realize, there are innumerable destinations to choose from. I wouldn't pretend to know your friend better than you do, but I think there's a pattern."

"Lucy wasn't a hoarder," I said. "When we took a trip she collected all the research beforehand, then threw most of it away after we got back." I was starting to convince myself. "These must've been places she intended to visit."

"I agree."

I couldn't wholeheartedly believe she'd left these pamphlets for me to find, but they were all I had to go on.

"But I don't know where to begin to look."

"You have to look everywhere."

"It'll take me ages to work up the technique to handle journeys like this. Her trail will have gone cold by then."

"So you're going to need my help," said Walt Whitman.

II

THE JOURNEY

A CAFÉ ON THE BOSPHORUS

In the afterlife the fashionable restaurants can be crowded. Reservations must be made in person, as there is no telephone service. In nearly every era taverns are particularly exuberant along the much-trodden pilgrimage routes.

Any 19th century foray should include absinthe; similarly, no trip to Asia should omit an opium den. A wise traveler will leave his moral criticism at the door.

The golden age of cafés stretches from the mid-18th century to the early 20th. The visitor enjoying their well-thumbed gazettes must bear in mind that these are artifacts of a prior world, of no more relevance here than the cups or saucers.

At all such establishments the conviviality can be misleading. In the afterlife there arises a natural fellowship among strangers, but this should not be mistaken for friendship. Indeed, the only way to escape past transgressions, the unavoidable hurt of loved ones, the wound that cannot be bandaged up by eternity, the pain that cannot ever be forgiven, is to return to mortality and begin anew as someone else.

"That damned tablet of guile," muttered Whitman.

We were standing outside Lucy's building, in brisk Manhattan sunlight. He indicated the guidebook filling my jacket pocket.

"I've only glanced at the thing."

He said, "I suppose someone offered it to you as a gift. Or else you found it bedside your first day."

"That's right."

He shook his shaggy head. "I often pose myself a conundrum. Which books have done the most evil in the world? The prior world. Religious tracts? So-called philosophy? History written with a hidden motive? All of it balanced by poetry."

It was easy to see him beavering away at his lists, crossing off his candidates, reordering them, scribbling new ones, discarding, starting over.

"Congratulations," I said. "I had trouble telling students which recordings to buy. I'd tell them to go to the library and check out everything."

"However," he went on imperviously, "there was never any doubt, on strong evidence, which criminal in the afterlife has had the most pernicious effect on innocent readers. Guidebook? Travel tips? It's nothing less than mind control."

I wondered when we'd get to Lucy. "The 20th century called it advertising."

"Is that so?" he said good-naturedly. "Let me remind you, my friend, I lived in the 20th century longer than you. Yes, I do call the afterlife living. And I do not call that book advertising. Now, where should we look?"

"Two mistakes. I should've left her a note upstairs, in case she turns up. And I need a photo of her, to show people."

"I have in my pocket a more useful volume, her passport, which contains a very attractive picture. If you like, you can keep it in your own pocket. Close to your heart, I suggest, and as far as possible from that evil propaganda. No, don't throw the guide-book away; I want you to study it when you know more."

I took her old navy-blue passport from him, and there she was, as I'd met her: so much vibrant youth, so much dynamic health, the promise of nearly twenty years together. What was the lesson, that love turns out to be a victim of mathematics? The number of happy years life gives you, like the number of paces you're allotted to cross a room before you collapse?

"I still can't stomach the thought of her coming back and not realizing I'm looking for her. I left her a note in our apartment."

"I promise, I won't let us miss her," said Walt. "It's impossible here to duplicate oneself timewise by being two places at once, but believe me, if she returns, I shall be informed. Did any of her travel pamphlets seem most likely?"

"That's the problem. She could be anywhere."

"Oh," he said, "there are some places she'd never venture. Not at this point in her experience. But I'll explain those in good time."

A siren should've started keening for me at that moment.

"I don't know where to begin," I said lamely.

He put his hand on my shoulder. "Don't lose faith," he intoned. "Nobody knows how she thinks better than you. Besides—don't take this the wrong way—people are surprisingly predictable. Even after they arrive. That's their mystery, and their beauty. People always remain themselves. Except when they go back."

In front of us midday traffic flowed like a grotesque insult. Those cars knew where they were going; taxis were ready to take us if I could only decide where.

"Ask her," said my companion softly, "*where are you now?*"

People who never speak of having a sixth sense or second sight or flashes of instinct will, in a crisis, decide they're clairvoyant.

Lose your keys, shut your eyes, then picture where they are—presto! Laundry hamper, jeans, back pocket. But I wasn't a mind reader, and I don't misplace my keys.

"Istanbul." I opened my eyes. "Or five blocks from here. Who knows?"

"Istanbul it is," said Walt Whitman. "Any particular era?"

"No idea." Needle in a timestack.

"No time like the present. I know a fine coffeehouse. Step right this way."

One instant we were crossing Duane Street, the next we were blasted with sunlight off a dancing strait of blue waves. Beyond rose green hills and a rounded medieval tower. A sluggish trolley belled as we penetrated the old-fashioned cars hooting and clattering along the coast road. When we finally achieved the other side, Walt said, "They drive like Turks around here! It's summer, 1964. Your Lucy would prefer it then. Like the rest of Istanbul, my café ends up going downhill and gets abysmally restored. No excuse, since they have only to go see how it looked."

He was chatting away as if it were as normal as a nap to take two steps and arrive somewhere you'd never been, under a fresh sky.

"So we're in a miniature golden age. A lovely area called Bebek. There's an American college here, in fact, with a Whitman course. I sometimes audit, for fun."

Before us a couple of enormous oil tankers were inching up the Bosphorus toward the Black Sea. There were few large boats, only a couple of chubby ferries crisscrossing to the right where the city began its sprawl. We were in Europe; those hills on the other side were Asia. I knew that much.

The other continent looked close enough to swim to, less than a mile. This was the sort of stunt Lucy might try, to prove she could do it. It was easy to imagine her inquiring: "Where's the best current? It's not against the law, is it?"

Maybe I should ask these two old men on a bench, eating kebab out of folded newspapers, if they'd seen an American woman backstroking between tankers?

"Go ahead," said Walt. "You never know."

"I don't speak Turkish. They don't look as if they speak English."

"They speak English whenever they have to. Better yet, you do speak Turkish. You simply don't accept it. Time to start your education."

He practically shoved me forward.

I approached them, nodded politely, and said in passable Turkish, "I'm sorry to bother you, sirs, but I'm looking for someone. I wonder if you might have seen her on a sunny day like today." I described her—remembering how fit she looked in a bikini—surprised at how natural it felt to do so in an unknown language. I found I knew the words for *brown-haired* and *dimples*. "She might've gone swimming."

One man said, "When I was her age I used to swim across every day for lunch. It was half the price on the other side, you know. That was before the war."

"You didn't take the ferry?" I asked.

"Why pay those robbers when I could swim?" He snapped his fingers.

The other man said, "I would swim across every Sunday. There was a girl who worked in a teashop on the other side. I liked how she looked at me. I was very athletic in those days. You wouldn't know it to look at me now."

I understood them effortlessly.

"What happened to the girl?" said the first. He winked, to show he knew.

"I married her." The other smiled. "She never stopped looking at me. But we sure got old together!"

"And my friend?" I asked.

"What did you say her name was?"

"Lucy."

They looked at each other as if trying to decide whose whiskers grew slowest.

The first man said, "There was a Suzy. Are you sure her name wasn't Suzy?"

"I'm pretty sure." I mentioned how she could outswim a tugboat. Then I remembered, pulled out her passport, showed them her youthful photo.

"I think that's her. She looked a bit older. It was a few years ago."

"How many?"

"Five? Ten? Hard to say."

"We've been sitting here a long time!"

"She was a strong swimmer, all right. I remember—" He pointed. "We told her to go in over there. You'd be surprised. Thirty meters round the bend, the current takes you across like a baby. She listened to us, too!"

"Did you ever see her again?"

"That was the remarkable thing," said the second man. "She was very polite, especially for an American. She came back the next day to thank us for giving her such wise advice. She even brought us a couple of beers."

Yes, that was Lucy.

"I don't suppose she told you where she was going next."

"I think she said she was going to get a coffee."

After I thanked them I rejoined Whitman in a grove of trees, and we started strolling again beside the Bosphorus. "You should be cheered by this," he said. "I can't think of a better vindication of your instincts."

"Five years ago, they said. Ten years ago. She's only been dead for four."

"Those dates," he said mildly, "could be merely her yesterday."

"Got it."

Just before she died she'd made clear there was nothing outstanding between us, to be forgiven from either side. But facing death, you say things to assuage the living that—especially in retrospect—you don't mean. Here she seemed to be living her own life entirely, with no gestures in my direction. Remember how frustrating it is, when you're young, to have a girlfriend avoid you? Multiply that by eternity.

We were coming to a thriving harbor sprinkled with sailboats and fishing dories, several restaurants and food stands, a mosque, a tailor's, a newspaper kiosk, a few cafés, even a chocolate shop into which he led me. A balding, mustached fellow in a jacket many decades out of fashion bustled over. "Mr. Whitman! Always a pleasure. Your usual table?"

We shook hands and Walt, in decorous Turkish, asked after our host's relatives as we were ushered to a terrace table beside the lapping water. A couple of tiny coffees, thick as quicksand, appeared from a reverent waiter along with a plate of chocolates shaped like flowers. So Walt Whitman had a sweet tooth, who knew?

"If I ever have to wait out another war," he said, "I believe I'll do it in Istanbul. This is the omphalos, the center of all things. And if aliens ever arrive, looking to commandeer a world capital to rule us from, I'll send them here."

"I assume there's no war in the Land of Later On?"

He bit into a black tulip. "You assume wrong."

"How can that be? Everyone's already dead."

"Therefore, what would be the point of war? You probably don't realize how many participated during your era in those fun Civil War reenactments. Everybody dresses up and lies down when they're shot. Then they have cookouts. They do the same here in the afterlife, except they truly mean it. They fight with all they've got."

"Who are they? War buffs? Historians?"

"The military buffs don't last, when confronted with the monstrosity. And scholars take all the lawlessness and animality and turn them into a quadrille for a ballroom. The real war never gets in the books. No, it's the original participants who try again. Young men who died for nothing. Old men who survived but want to be strong once more to avenge their comrades. Officers determined not to repeat their mistakes. If you want, you can savor the afterlife's current versions of every battle ever fought." He paused. "It's never the politicians who participate. The Civil War was Armageddon, I toured its hospitals. Nine hundred and ninety-nine parts diarrhea to one part glory. I always said the people who like the wars should be compelled to fight the wars. The sadness is how soldiers keep fighting to learn what they already know. Being dead gives them a convenient excuse, so men go back to waging their battles. Like a dog to its vomit."

To private conflicts, also?

"And you," said Walt conversationally, "how did you get here? I found one recording in Lucy's flat. It must've been strange, as a musician, to face that disease."

"Like I'd been dreaming my whole life. Then I woke up."

Strange didn't cover how it felt to lose the piano, to no longer be myself. I'd died years before my suicide.

"Still, a life to be envied." At my expression, he added, "I don't question your choice. One of my best friends cut his wrists. The question is what you do with yourself now that you're here. Suppose you can't find Lucy?"

Suppose she won't let me find her? "You don't think I will, do you."

"I didn't say that. But there's a kind of nakedness in such a search, and people are more comfortable clothed than naked."

Maybe he meant I'd give up easily.

"Is there a way for her to find out what happened to me?"

"Word filters through from the future. And gets passed around. She might run into someone who died after you did, who can tell her."

"That could take ages. I haven't been here very long."

"Nope," he said quietly, "you haven't. Time here is much more malleable, and more coincidental, than you realize. If the fellow who used to sell you a paper every morning shows up, and if Lucy chooses to visit Niagara Falls on the same day that he's there, he can tell her."

"She wouldn't visit Niagara Falls."

"You're very impatient. Have a chocolate, I'm eating all of them. You catch my point. I wouldn't discredit any possibility."

No doubt I did sound impatient, from his view across a timeless Bosphorus, but I felt an urgency in my bones I hadn't known since my disease made traipsing through each day a struggle. In youth that urgency had made me so dislike being a bad pianist that I became a fine one. I couldn't sense where Walt's own urgency lay, after more than a century in the Land of Later On. Nobody was going to dispute that he was a great poet, but surely it was time for another book, not more scribbled rewrites? Maybe he was scared to try something new.

Okay, that was none of my business, and I knew my place in the hierarchy; I was just a well-trained nightclub pianist with occasional flights for a tune here, a tune there. As Lucy said, one swallow does not a summer make.

"I don't see the plan," I said. "Do I explore Istanbul's past and future? Or try to figure out where she went next?"

He smiled. "You speak as if you have something more important to do."

"I'm a little daunted by the possibilities."

"And I don't blame you a bit. One lesson of the afterlife is that you learn to trust your instincts about people. I always did, and I was seldom wrong. Death has a way of refining character, making people more themselves than they were. The vaguenesses drop away. There's the surprise of finding somebody more interesting than you ever found them in life. Mostly you find you can predict where someone might be with more accuracy than you'd expect. After all, you didn't hope to stumble on Lucy's trail our first try, did you? I'm telling you this wasn't a stumble."

He made an almost indiscernible gesture and two waiters came running, jostling for the privilege of bringing us more coffees.

"Such eager young men. Look here." From a side pocket of his sailcloth shirt he pulled a wad of folded yellow paper and a cheap ballpoint pen. I watched him derive a child's satisfaction from clicking its button a couple of times. "What an invention. You have no idea what a nuisance its predecessors were."

There was the hoot of a ferry. He unfolded the rumpled paper. At the top he printed, in his immaculate hand, *Lucy's Expedition*, and underlined it.

"Now," he said, "let's say you're writing a poem. Pretend I'm not here—"

"How can I? I wouldn't be here if it weren't for you."

He smiled. "Walt Whitman, private secretary." I liked how he garnered so much amusement from his own jokes. "What I mean is this: I always used to tell myself I was writing my poetry for the dearest, closest friend I could conceive. Someone who'd never existed but whom I could imagine intimately. It was only through such a friend that I could envision speaking to the world. Had I worried what strangers might think, I'd never have written a line. And I'm sure whenever you play the piano you've found a way of speaking inwardly that still opens out. So I need you to tell me where Lucy, your Lucy, would go. Where you think she might be happy, knowing you'll find her there one day."

WHY YOU MIGHT NOT WANT
TO KEEP READING

For most of my life, as for so many, the prospect of dying seemed far away. Lucy and I couldn't have children, and we'd made our peace with that—maybe if we had started trying earlier we'd have considered adopting. It was natural to visualize growing old together, and it seemed cruel that one of us, some distant winter, would die first and leave the other in isolation.

What was unimaginable was that it might happen soon. I loved my life with Lucy, I wanted it to go on and on. Through great determination and talent she had prospered as a private yoga teacher; she'd long ago been able to quit part-time work in flower shops. And she was writing a health, diet, and exercise book before she got ill. I too was making an acceptable living at my own difficult gig. I was proud of what my playing had become, an ability I'd bought from my body with hard work. I planned to keep recording: solo discs, duos, trios. Even though my career was mainly East Coast, I had a reputation in the most rigorous jazz city in the world. I certainly never thought of myself as a candidate for early retirement.

After about age thirty-nine, none of it went as we hoped—nothing unusual in the second half of a life turning out much worse than the first half. I chose, with the minimal independence I had left, to try doing something about it.

You might conclude that the Land of Later On is filled with people who successfully (it's not as easy as I expected, to state the obvious) hanged themselves, blew off the backs of their heads, jumped from skyscraper ledges or high bridges, threw their bodies in front of trains, fell on their swords, stood under trees in electric storms, went surfing in hurricanes, poisoned or syringed themselves—the list is endless, the statistics of failure sobering. But suicides are like everyone else: they get to the afterlife, skim the guidebook or listen to shaky advice, miss some element of their lives which suddenly matters now that the overriding pain is removed, then realize they can start again from scratch . . . and without assessing the consequences, they toodle back before you can offer them a coffee. (I promise you haven't tasted coffee till you've died and gone to heaven.) Some days it strikes you as sad, some days it just seems pathetic.

Anyway, I've made my point—that unless you truly can't abide remaining who you were, you should not give in to yearnings to go back. Above all, you must not trust the guidebook's "well-meaning" wisdom. I did not grasp the intricate warp and weft of its ambition until Whitman revealed them, subterfuge upon subterfuge, as we leaped oceans and centuries together in search of my Lucy.

Like many musicians, able to play much more deeply than we can speak or even think, my sense of intimacy had been measured among colleagues. Jazzers can be shy to the point of becoming inarticulate, but when we're on the stand, working together for a common good, making it up rapidly out of an apparent nothingness, the music conjured from blank air and doomed to vanish as soon as it exists, we say things to each other that we never would any other way. Off the stand we're pals; making music, we're lovers. The jointly improvised sound enables our intimacy as nothing else ever could. And, best of all, lovers with nothing to prove, who trust each other totally, who look after each other's welfare no matter what goes wrong.

I never felt that playing jazz was a substitute for a close relationship. But though I had my share of girlfriends, until I met Lucy I'd never been with a woman so unconditionally. After a couple of months, our shared lives beneath the covers became a perfect enclosed universe in which sometimes we were not certain whose limbs were whose. There was more unity in our arguments about much that didn't matter than in any more harmonious affair either of us had ever had. It takes time, but eventually your ear tells you the right dissonant chord is far more beautiful, ultimately more satisfying, than the obvious consonant ones.

There's a classic bossa nova called *Insensetaz*, by Antônio Carlos Jobim, which gets translated as *How Insensitive*. Jazz musicians love to improvise on the tune because of the ambiguity of its episodes; it seems to float through several keys at once, and the internal voices have their own tug and drift. Though civilians don't notice, it's based closely on that Chopin prelude I was playing at the bank when Lucy and I met. She, being an unusually astute listener, heard the resemblance, and often asked me to move from one poignant piece to the other.

It was much on my mind several months before she died because I came back from a three-week Caribbean jazz cruise and a solo version I'd recorded was playing in our apartment. She'd been diagnosed only six months earlier but gone down fast, changed from being an unstoppable force to someone who looked doomed. She was always a person who took in the world primarily through physical sensation; it was her barometer of truth, and now she couldn't accept that her body was betraying her.

Our plan had been to go away together, aware of what was coming, but when the offer came in from four musicians I scarcely knew to complete their group, I grabbed the gig with my good hand. I was capable of what little I'd have to do to get by—no solos, I warned them. The money was adequate, we certainly needed it, and I knew it was the last gasp of my career. Ordinarily I'd have brought her along, but it seemed crazy to waste her energy. We'd head to the Southwest on my return, rent a car, take our sweet time. That stupid cruise would pay for half our trip.

We'd been joking about what a traveling pair we'd make. My right side had been increasingly wonky and I'd stopped playing professionally a while ago, but I could still limp around easily with a cane. A sprained ankle slowly healing, you'd think, not a serious neurological disorder.

I was surprised to find her prone in darkness rather than out for a walk or doing her own yoga practice; from the first diagnosis she'd been determined to beat her illness, to last as long as possible in full health. One of her tenets was that diet and exercise could handle almost anything. She'd begun taking longer naps during the afternoon, but when I called every few days from the ship she told me she felt she was doing better. A couple of friends were taking her on daily walks, she was doing all her own grocery shopping, she was even giving a few lessons again in our living room. These were phony press releases to reassure me, and they worked.

I knew this as soon as I walked in, exhausted from a three-stop trajectory from Miami, via Chicago, that ate the afternoon. Our flat smelled like decay and worse. *How Insensitive* was playing, the title wasn't lost on me, and I could hear her loud breathing in the darkened bedroom. She was wide awake and bleary-eyed.

"You're back," she said.

"Sorry, it took me an eternity to get here from Florida."

"Lickety-Split." Her voice was quiet.

I sat down on the bed and took her hand. "I shouldn't have gone."

"Did they pay you?"

"Every centime. Every ruble."

"I guess it was worth it, then."

She was looking up at the ceiling, not at me.

"And did you play okay?"

"Pretty abysmally. I got by. But I won't make that mistake again."

"It's all right."

"Can I make you something to eat? You've lost weight."

"I never understood," she said, "how much this song means. Until the last few weeks. You must've always known. Otherwise you wouldn't play it so well."

"We've got to get your strength back up. We can leave for Arizona as soon as you like. There's nothing stopping us from going."

Then she did look at me. "You know," she murmured, "you'd be surprised."

LUCY'S EXPEDITION

It was not (I imagined her saying to herself) *that I didn't want Kip to find me, but I wasn't going to just wait for years and years around the apartment I died in.*

The great mystery here is the relation people have to themselves— why so many choose to return and become someone else. Why others stick around.

Being dead asks you to decide if you're a clumsy prototype who would be improved by going back. Smelting yourself in humanity's furnace. Meaning that all who choose to stay in the Land of Later On are, at heart, arrogant? And selfish? If so, count me in, since Kip is bound to show up sooner or later.

This at least was what I hoped Lucy was saying. Walt sat with ballpoint pen hovering, expecting me to come up with her magical list, while I wished there were some upright in a corner so I could play a bit and think.

He waited, gazing across the harbor at men unloading baskets of silver sardines from their dories and bickering with other men waving fistfuls of money from the dock. Finally he said, "You know, it doesn't cost anything to search. The worst that can happen is we don't find her at first. My suggestion"—he cleared his throat to show he was merely offering free advice—"is we start with the pamphlets. We might not need to go very far down her list."

"I don't see why you're helping me."

"I'm your friend."

"I'm grateful, but we barely know each other." Plus you have no idea why Lucy might be avoiding me. Even trying to forget me.

"But I believe you need my help." He hesitated. "And it has struck me, in my months at Lucy's apartment, that she must've been very special. A person's bookshelves rarely mislead. Painful as it is to admit, the thing that touched me most in my prior time, and in my time here, has been the long faithfulness of lovers."

He was all but inaudible over the shushing waters.

He said, "Nothing else in life made me so envious, so bitter, so admiring, because I never was fortunate enough to enjoy it for long. Whenever I come into contact, it's as cleansing as the smell of the sea. I honor it by doing whatever I can to help. Better than scratching out endless rewrites no one will ever read."

When Lucy first moved in, without any pact for the future, it felt as natural as spending weekends at each other's flat. I didn't have a lot of stuff—I've always been a supporter of public librar-ies—so apart from building her another bookcase, or buying a chest of drawers larger than a man alone would need, or replac-ing some cheap kitchen gear I used on the nights I wasn't eating on the job, it was easy to make room. Throughout eighteen years we never discussed getting married, I guess because after around 1990 it seemed obvious we'd stay together. Neither of us had any family to please with a ceremony, and we already felt allied against the solitude of the world. A lawyer advised us we were fools not to draw up wills; she told him, "We plan to live forever, and we already have a joint bank account." We followed most of his counsel but neglected to buy life insurance.

I watched Walt scribbling with authority those place names off the pamphlets he'd shown me. His handwriting was simultaneously elegant yet relaxed, some letters angular, some curved, the words linked with enormous propulsion. And organized, as if Walt were writing on lined paper even when he wasn't.

For some reason his purposeful handwriting made me question why he was ready to spend so much time trying to help. I said, "Are there many like you here?"

"Poets who stuck around? Remarkably few. The deeply Christian ones, like Mr. Milton, or a man I hoped would be my friend, Mr. Blake, found the truth too jarring. And for Signore Dante the whole experience was a severe form of literary criticism. Every one of us, of course, dreamed of meeting Shakespeare, but he let his human enthusiasm get the better of his judgment. Now none will know him."

He'd misunderstood me, so I played along. "Lord Byron?"

Whitman chuckled. "Oh, he's still here. At his most handsome. Let's say he has one thing on his mind, and it's not revision. By and large, continentals have an easier time accepting the Land of Later On. In my day we thought them romantic compared to the Anglo-Saxon tradition, but it turns out they're much more sensible. You can meet Goethe, Lorca, even Sappho, whenever you want. Pushkin's produced his best work posthumously—that's one man's opinion. We sometimes meet at this very café, though he prefers it in winter. Must be the Russian blood."

"I don't suppose you're all in this underground organization."

"We come from many walks of life."

"And your goal is—?"

THE LAND OF LATER ON

"Persuading people to be more patient in making up their minds to return. That guidebook is only the most egregious form of propaganda. Many are swayed by a vapor in the air, the faint mood of repentance. Or a lack of customary gadgets. It's often enough to demonstrate how much enjoyment may be had from a wealth of time. Everybody does his part. Your neighbor Billy is one of us, by the way."

"You're joking."

"Not at all. He had an ancestor who was an effective spy in my era. During the war of secession. Belle Boyd."

"I never imagined Billy as a joiner. Or—how would you put it?—selfless."

He shook his head. "Pornography's an eloquent way to show people there's amusement to be found in the afterlife. The erotic makes a welcome tonic for almost any loss. And I don't think being high-minded is an effective way to convince anybody of anything. If money were useful we'd hand out bribes."

"Are there many in your cabal?"

"Not enough." He noticed I was looking at him askance. "This is partly why I want you to find Lucy. I hope you'll both help us one day. If that makes you trust me, more than to believe I'm here out of the charity of my heart, very well."

"That wasn't what I meant. I keep wondering what lies behind all this. Who's in charge? Who wrote the guidebook? And makes sure every newcomer gets a copy?"

He didn't look the slightest bit guilty for finishing the chocolates. "The author—authors?—wish to remain anonymous. I'm not surprised. And are they responsible for *all* this? Or hired wordsmiths? You'd think we'd know, but we don't. Even during my own span here, the afterlife has changed. Grown smothered in shameless scheming. The message of the guidebook assumes innumerable forms. All a shrewd disproof of the joys everyone finds on arrival. Why explore the bounty of this sweet wide world in your own good time, earned out of a hundred incarnations you don't remember, when you can purchase the same hemlock as before?"

"I don't follow you."

He grabbed my arm—a strong grip for a dead man. "Too many people are choosing to stay. No wonder you're supposed to leave immediately! No wonder they bully you to return! They're running out of personalities!"

"Doesn't make sense," I said. "The population of the earth has gone up by two billion, or something, in my lifetime."

"And hence their greater need." Whitman held my arm like there was no tomorrow. "You speak as if it's the former world which matters. You've got it backward. The life you endured before arriving was a crude training encampment to prepare you for the struggle ahead." His eyes blazed. "It's not as if there isn't plenty of room *here*. The problem is more and more people gradually being born *there*. And fewer and fewer from here going back. Mechanisms were put in place. Like our treacherous guidebook. Half-truths are more misleading, more fatal, than outright lies. So that's what the guidebook deals in. To seduce hapless readers, via helpful warnings, into buying malicious falsehoods." He let my arm go, frowned. "If you believe in the individuality of the soul, as I do, you'll agree it's better if people aren't conned into going back. This should be where one learns the truth." He closed his eyes. "I'm boring you."

"Look, my mind isn't on lofty goals, all that interests me is getting to Lucy." I nearly said *apologizing*. Was Istanbul where one learned the hard truth? "Sorry to disappoint you."

"I wouldn't expect you to desert the cause." He smiled. "Don't worry, she is my cause at the moment." He glanced at the list, stuffed it in his pocket. Like his poetry, he was all over the place. "Tell me, have you ever been to India?"

"I haven't. Lucy often talked about going, though."

He pointed past me at the Bosphorus dories unloading. "Isn't it always a wonder how many fish can come out of one sea?" He reached across the café table to grasp my arm again. At that instant I felt the shimmering which meant we were on our way to somewhere and somewhen else. I turned in my chair, though, to see where he was pointing, and inadvertently I must've pulled away.

The shimmering ceased. I was elsewhere, it sure wasn't India, and I was alone.

A SERIOUS MISSTEP

It is all too easy, transferring across centuries and tracts of longitude and latitude, to make a serious misstep and wind up far from the intended destination. The unfortunate traveler might find himself pressed into servitude or even slavery, military danger, extreme youth or old age, radical poverty and abject starvation, physical anguish, et cetera. Only the same feat of imagination which brought the traveler here can effect an escape; belief in the ability to do so is crucial.

Also to be borne in mind is that a newcomer will find it less unnatural to shift to the locales of one's past or to destinations previously imagined in detail. The hobbyist obsessed, for example, with the Austro-Hungarian Empire may have little difficulty accomplishing a visit. For the traveler to reach an unfamiliar place and time is much more complex. Finding a way back is arduous; the risks are grave.

And if that doesn't frighten the daylights out of you, I don't know what will.

How, you ask, did I know I wasn't in India, since I'd never been there? Was it the absence of elephants and tigers, or bazaars and temples and saris? Was it a growing sense that I didn't know what on earth I was doing? Or the fact that my guide was no longer beside me, and since he did know what he was doing and must be in India, that meant I wasn't?

Where I was was a kind of green hell of maniacal vegetation on all sides. The air was clammy, and my clothes stuck to me as if I'd been sweating for days. I've never seen a tropical jungle, but I was pretty sure I was in one, since I was wading in swamp mud to my knees and leeches were attacking me above the boots I hadn't been wearing by the Bosphorus a minute ago. From somewhere to the right, about a mile away, came muffled bursts of machine-gun fire. I was suddenly aware I was carrying a heavy rifle in both hands, with a pack strapped to my back. As this awareness hit, I staggered.

Relative silence, except for the screech of birds and some frog going off like an alarm clock. The steady suck of my boots, the giveaway rattle and cough of my equipment—what could be more inviting to an alert sniper?—and my own asthmatic wheeze as I plodded along. I've never had a good sense of smell, but one stench was overpowering. Not jungle, but of a man who hadn't washed any part of himself properly, much less his clothes, in weeks. All around, though I sensed rather than heard or saw them, were my comrades. What kept going through my head was a phrase I didn't understand: *Buna, bloody Buna, bloody goddamned Buna.*

My comrades: there were four. Peering through dappled jungle light I found them, like points of the compass. Josie, Hiram, the Stickman, and Benjy. I knew there were relative ranks among us, but at the moment what mattered was whether the Japanese machine-gunner who'd successfully hidden behind an enormous fallen tree trunk on the trail ahead was back this afternoon.

One by one we pulled ourselves out of the muck and formed up on dry land, then fanned out again, heading for what we'd come to call the Log. I was third to get clear of the swamp, but now I was the only grunt on the actual trail.

It didn't help to remind myself I was in no danger of getting killed; Billy's rant about dead dictators suffering intense physical

torment came back loud and clear. Suppose machine-gun fire
ripped through the trees and tore me apart? Even if I couldn't die,
I wasn't meant to be here. Lucy sure wasn't hanging around here.

None of us saw the enemy when the attack finally came. Probably the Log was now a ruse to keep us looking ahead, not high
in the indecipherable branches that were a sniper's headquarters.
Josie, to my left, went over without a word, at one shot. Immediately after, the Stickman crumpled groaning on the second shot.

I forgot about the others and threw myself behind the fattest
tree nearby, praying it was between me and the sniper. I told myself
that my two dead comrades were not dead—this was the afterlife, they'd pull through in the end, right? Enemy bullets might've
caught them by surprise, but it didn't count in the Land of Later
On. Yet why the fuck were grown men forcing themselves to go
through this?

A couple of shots—ours, not theirs—thudded up ahead.
There was an enormous pause, lasting ten seconds, as the sniper's
harness must've sagged and given way. We heard a prolonged swish
(I remember thinking: *What's so beautiful about that?*—even while
it seemed inexpressibly lyrical) and the chunky impact of a falling
body hitting the jungle floor.

"Another asswipe meets his Emperor," said Hiram loudly.

I laid down my rifle and put my head in my hands, biting
the fabric of my stinking shirt, sucking my own sweat from the
military cotton. I realized abruptly that I could guess where I was:
New Guinea, sometime in World War II. I knew I should get up
and go tend to my shot comrades. Or maybe they were standing already, laughing, brushing off the dirt? Helping up the sniper
who'd toppled out of the trees, rifle in hand, bullets through his
throat and forehead? I didn't hear anybody laughing, I didn't hear
anybody helping anybody.

"Safe to advance," said Benjy, twenty yards in front, and I don't think it was my paranoia that detected a sneer in his voice. I was trying to remember exactly what Whitman had said about battles, something about a dog and its vomit. Could these men really be here voluntarily? I tried furiously to imagine myself somewhere else, tried to summon the blurry sensation of shifting I'd undergone nearly twenty times now. Shift, I yelled silently, shift, dammit! But my desperation wasn't doing me any good. In one pocket of my fatigues I could feel the familiar presence of the guidebook, could easily imagine what it would say: *Tough luck, asswipe. If you'd listened to me, you wouldn't be here. Want out? There's an easy way.*

Music saves you at the most unexpected times. From seemingly far off I had an acute memory of what it'd felt like, too often, improvising and finding myself in a place where I didn't know the proper harmony of the tune—I couldn't hear a route through the thicket of notes I was producing, the path from bar five to bar seven was vague. This bypasses a listener in seconds, unnoticed, but to a musician it happens in vivid slow-motion. There's no solution except experience; when you improvise a lot and can relax on an instrument, a hundred possibilities occupy your head at any moment. If something goes wrong you're able to pluck another possibility out of the air in a heartbeat, and the listener never knows. But if you tense up and let your panic get the better of you, you're doomed.

Easy to say after playing the piano forty years; I'd only been in the afterlife for days. I closed my eyes and told myself the sniper was out of business. I pretended there was nothing more enjoyable than leeches gorging on my calves, leaned against the tree, and thought of India. And Lucy, outfitted as a temple dancer.

"You can get up now," said Whitman.

The leeches were gone. The sunlit air still felt tropical, there was a tree at my back, but I was in regular clothes and couldn't smell my unwashed self anymore. Always a good sign.

"That was horrible," I said. "How long was I in the jungle?"

"About an hour."

He helped me up. We seemed to be in overgrown botanical gardens that ended in forested hillside, with a shattered stone staircase climbing through vines. There were lavish trees I recognized from Caribbean trips with Lucy. We were alone, and the paths looked riotous. Behind us loomed mountains thick with steaming vegetation. I had a strong feeling this was not the present, but a few centuries before. Just as some people uncannily know what time it is within minutes (my mother had this knack), after you've shifted a bit you acquire an intuition of what year or even day it is, even with no obvious clues in sight.

"An hour? That's it?"

He said impatiently, "While you were exploring jungle paths, I was busy leapfrogging through dozens of different locales and eras looking for you."

"Sorry to be such a nuisance."

"Oddly enough, the swamps of Papua New Guinea around Christmas 1942 weren't the first place I thought of. Until it occurred to Billy Boyd that a clue to your whereabouts might be found with one of your relatives."

"I don't understand."

Afternoon heat curdled the air. Beyond Whitman were flowering red poinciana trees and a gunmetal-gray sea.

"Was Buna a passion of yours?" he asked.

"I doubt I can even find it on a map."

"Think of the experience as a kind of open-air university in the nature of time. And displacement."

"I don't get it."

"These submerged currents are powerful. You'll gauge them soon enough."

"Hang on," I said. "I did have an uncle on my father's side, who was wounded at the battle of Buna. I never met him, but—"

"That's how the idea got seeded. Luckily Billy remembered your mentioning this once and suggested you might've made some unwitting tropical association with the idea of India. Let's hope to God you didn't have an ancestor at Gettysburg. Perhaps you have heard that it is good to gain the day, but battles are won in the same bleakness of spirit in which they are lost."

"And where are we now?"

Whitman said, "Dominica. 1796. In what was once the British West Indies. We're in the gardens outside a small port called Roseau. A favorite place of mine in this part of the world, in later centuries. One of those islands that tourism passes by, because the beaches are black and volcanic. Not white and powdery."

"Was this island in Lucy's drawer?"

"I did find a pamphlet. From around now. Your Lucy seems to have been historically inclined. I doubt she'll have stayed long. Nevertheless, worth a try."

"But you don't believe she's here anymore."

"Probably not. Think of it as part of your education."

A low stone wall ran beside the unkempt gardens. Clouds were approaching in battle formation out of the swollen horizon of sea. Below us the town of wooden buildings was painted in yellows and reds and blues. We went through a gap in the stone wall to a road.

I tried to imagine her stunned surprise, then *What took you so long?*, followed by her familiar arms clasping my neck. I thought:

I don't want to be educated, I don't want to be shot at even if it doesn't count, I want to find Lucy.

"And so we shall," said Walt. "But there are places on her list which I do not think worth a serious investigation, and I want to show you why. I would rather not hazard your distrust. It may be I'm wrong. It may be you'll tell me these are the very places we most must look. Anyway"—he took my elbow—"we aren't going to walk, not in this heat."

Once again that shifting sensation, as if my entire body blinked. I knew we were still on Dominica, the same year, the very same day. An interior gyroscope steadied itself and told me we'd traveled about five miles. Now we were walking down a road toward the interior. Steep canyons fell away to rain forests gone mad with growing; from their depths came garbled cries of birds. The palms and the banana trees appeared so dense that no one could live in them, but as we walked I noticed a cosmos of trails, and shacks coughing smoke.

Above us the volcanic mountains rose, plum-colored in the mists. At every twist in the road I glimpsed a waterfall charging down pillars of fern-covered rock. Then the bosom of mountains parted so a canyon lay revealed. I saw below us, perhaps a mile away, the gray stone buildings of a sugar mill and its dependencies. I recognized the subservient shapes from a month I'd done at a boutique hotel (lousy piano, despite the hype) on one of those French islands. At first I thought this sugar plantation was abandoned, then I glimpsed figures squirming, at work.

"A noble sight, from a suitable distance, no?" said Walt softly. "Industrious mankind, undaunted by nature's splendor. Let's try a closer look."

Remarkable to be able to get around so easily: one instant we were above, gazing down into the canyon, the next we were standing beside the stone sugar mill. It was decrepit. We were not alone, but the figures I'd glimpsed from afar were, I realized, children—pushing carts of burlap sugar sacks, dragging iron tools through the dirt, chucking a bedraggled horse to persuade it to pull an overloaded wagon. Most were black, but there were white kids, too. Listless and filthy, all were in rags.

"And so, dear friend," Walt whispered, "your higher learning begins at last."

At first I couldn't speak. Though I'd seen a few very poor countries, I hadn't witnessed child labor like this. Not even on the news. They took no notice of us.

"What on earth are they doing here?" I managed. "What is this place?"

"This is the afterlife."

"Why don't they leave?"

"They don't know how. They don't know any different."

"Can't we explain to them—"

"You don't understand," he said gently. "These are the slaves my colleagues and I have failed to convince. At one point there were hundreds of adults and children at this very spot, serving this beleaguered mill. Thousands upon thousands slaved throughout these islands, and you can multiply it for our own country. After death, many returned to the sole place they knew."

"But why did they come back as children?"

"Because they died here as children. They could age, of course, anywhere they like, but they instinctively choose not to."

"So they're going to stay here as children forever?" I was stupefied. "Can't we bring them with us?"

"You can't kidnap people in the afterlife. I'm not speaking morally—I mean it just doesn't work. In a scientific sense. No matter how adept you may be, if you take the hand of that little girl and she doesn't want to come with you, she won't. I promise you, if it were otherwise this place would've been deserted long ago."

"What if another child came back—someone their own age, or slightly older—or their parents—tried to persuade them—"

"Do you take us for fools? Don't you think we've tried everything we can? Why do you suppose they pay no attention to the fact I'm here? They've seen me before, they've heard us out. We've brought them proper food, medical care. They accept it all stoically. These are the ones we've failed to rescue from slavery, who were indoctrinated too young and will remain in it as children forever. Unless they give up, go back, and start again. That's a difficult choice for a child. Yet we hold out hope, always, that we can persuade a few here, a few there, to accompany us to where they can be looked after. We've even tried promising we'll take them to their parents. Yet how are we to find their parents in all this confusion? Why should they still be alive in the Land of Later On? It's hopeless."

It looked pretty much like hell, and I said so.

"You won't hear an argument from me," said Walt quietly. "I wanted you to see this horror because I have an inkling your Lucy might've seen it, too. I want to assure you that there are many such places in the past where we need not bother to look. That she'd have surely investigated early in her journeyings. I doubt she would ever come back again."

I saw her staying a few days, trying to help, giving up in despair. Or perhaps Walt was wrong, perhaps she'd only ever visited places she could love, and was patiently running down those pamphlets. I hoped so, for her sake. There was nothing to be done here, not even in the afterlife.

What kept nagging away, beneath my visceral sadness, was remembering annoyed conversations I'd had with pretentious musicians who mocked the blues, who disdained the form's sense of inherited pain, claiming its "simplicity" was beneath them. They could choke on their wordy theories; sweating to my fingertips, I was staring at the roots of the blues in the forlorn eyes of an imported African child.

"And who are the white kids?" I asked.

"Those should be our allies. They're a great rarity. They're the ones who ran these places, who were adults once. Overseers who died of fever. Or wealthy owners, who reclined in their home countries. But they died, like everyone else, and when they got to the afterlife they decided to look at their old dominions. And what they saw made a difference, to a few. As a gesture of penitence they incorporated themselves here as children, slaving pointlessly away alongside those they murdered."

"So why don't they get the other children to leave?"

"Because they've come permanently. For the duration. They've been here a long time already, for several unchanging centuries. By now they've forgotten that they originally came out of choice. I suppose it's part of their psychological cure for such an unavenged crime. But they can't escape their instinct for cruelty. They tell the other kids our advice can't be trusted. That we're not human."

Before us two black boys, who looked barely nine, were struggling to lift a lumpen rock to fill a gap in the side of the sugar mill. A younger white boy and a little black girl were stirring a trough of mortar. The air was pocked with flies.

"I've seen enough," I said. "Let's get out of here."

A BREAK

The harshest of many harsh truths of the Land of Later On is that, while your stay in the afterlife lasts for as long as you choose, there is no decay of memory. No one's regrets disappear, and nostalgia for a former existence, strengthened by the afterlife's mirror, can be devastating.

This book isn't what I intended. My original idea was impersonal—advice for when your time comes. I even toyed with printing the thing myself (you can't take it with you and don't need money there anyway), then hiring gigless musicians to sell them at subway entrances for pocket change. My own Salvation Army. I can already hear some genius urging me to post it on the Web, a cyberspace equivalent of finding the guidebook bedside. My opinion is that the living take more seriously something they spent fifty cents on than something they get for nothing.

But it's become *only* personal, I see. As Whitman warned, sometimes you have to tell the entire story so that one peep of truth filters through.

So let me make it plain where I find myself writing this, and will no longer be by the time you read it: back in the rent-controlled mousehole Lucy and I shared all those years. Imagine it in a sweltering August, a fan creaking away, with the same spinet I left in the Land of Later On except that I can no longer play it and, being here, it sounds dinky again. My right hand a deformed pirate's hook I can unfurl only by dragging it across a table. Summer gunk on everything, the urban dust of ash, human skin, pigeon droppings. My cane by my side, since I can't cross my tiny south wing without it. Being unwillingly brought back to life seems to have encouraged my disease, though I plan to have the last laugh.

Suicide, even if only temporarily successful, does sort out the priorities. You might think my return would sprout strands of remorse. Friends I wished I'd said good-bye to, music I might've listened to one last time, the trash I forgot to take out. Since everybody shows up in the afterlife sooner or later—though you may never find them—and since you can hear any music you want there, that leaves only the trash.

If this sounds antisocial, too bad. Look, I sit dictating all day, dripping sweat on Lucy's desk, trying to get these pages over with so I can hurry back. Hardly the mood for conversation with close friends I avoided for years anyway. If I were to tell them my saga they'd have me committed, since other people know what's best for you; and it can't be convenient to dictate even a short book from a straitjacket. "The dilemma of editors," as Billy put it, I plan to sidestep. I'll dump this on every publisher in the city, whoever wants it first gets it free, and if more than one decides I'm not imagining things, the lawyers can sort it out.

The only person I miss back here, besides Lucy, is Billy. After her death, until he got too sick himself, we ate lunch together nearly every day; the schedules of a jazz musician and a writer suit each other perfectly. There's nobody like a pornographer to keep you from taking yourself seriously, and it was Billy who held me together for Lucy's illness and the next couple of years of anguish.

Their relationship was always a bit strained. She couldn't get past the fact he spent all day writing dirty books.

"It's his choice how he uses his talent," she said, "but let's not beat around the bush." She smiled winsomely. "They're who he is, they're what he does."

"Well, it's what he happens to be good at. Maybe he didn't choose it, maybe it chose him."

"So there's no free will? You and I didn't choose each other?"

"That's right."

"Then," she said, "I suppose we'll just have to take the pornographic with the sublime."

I did my best to return his kindness as cancer got the better of him. I'd water his plants and visit him in hospital, or accompany him to chemotherapy. Several times he sat there on a drip and amused himself scandalizing the other patients, hidden behind similar curtains in a circular room, as I read aloud the galleys of his latest filthy opus and made corrections for him, since his writing hand had a needle stuck in it delivering ten thousand dollars of liquid per hour.

"*She tore open her skintight space-sheath and shrieked, 'Take me! Take me in the most bestial way, Earthman! I want you to forge in the curvaceous smithy of my alien soul the new conscience of a sexually superhuman race!'*" I declaimed off the publisher's typeset pages.

"Kip, I'm not sure about *bestial*," he said dubiously. "Would an Amazon priestess from Venus use that word? I don't know, man. This chemo has upended my aesthetic compass."

"Trust your imagination, Billy."

"Easy for you to say. Some bastards have all the luck."

"My problem is that I'm not seeing her naked body vividly enough."

"Good point. All right, take this down: '*Her roused nipples were like titanium spear-points on the shield of some intergalactic...*'" Then would follow a paragraph of fortissimo excitement, and I would see him smile at the rustle of unseen fellow sufferers in armchairs nearby.

Here's a law of return that's possibly unique to me, because I came back as myself, right where I left. On being "saved" against your will, your readiness to see people is in inverse proportion to how much you care about them. The last friends I wanted to visit me were colleagues I'd worked with on hundreds of gigs. Apart from Lucy, these men shared the most treasured moments of my life; if you knew how to listen, we had virtually no secrets from each other. They respected that since we could no longer break musical bread together, I'd enlarged my distance over the years. It wasn't that I was jealous because they could still play, or didn't want to hear who they'd become. Nor that I didn't miss them enormously. But I couldn't imagine our friendship without my own contribution to what had been a wordless understanding. When we did run into each other on the street, I'd feel them searching my face for ulterior motives, since the choice was entirely mine. Yet I couldn't bear to talk about old times, or our profession, as a non-playing civilian. They'd stuck by me, keeping my income going as long as the charade could be maintained, filling in the gaps of my spastic right hand, telling me it sounded acceptable even when it didn't, putting up night after night with an ineptitude they'd never have tolerated from a clumsy newcomer. Until I went through that, I didn't realize what friendship can be.

Most frequent were two bassists. Nieske (rhymes with *pesky*) looked like a very tall owl and played like a first-rate composer (which he also was), everything in place, so stalwart, so loyal, you could be excused for not appreciating his ceaseless originality. His unfailing drive, like a steam engine, kept me going when my right hand ran out of strength. In his twenties he'd toured the world with one of the great reed players and assumed it would always be like that, international festivals and reviews, posters with his name on them. It takes guts to acknowledge that, no matter how much you've achieved, your performing life has leveled off.

The other was big, black, groovy Thomas, a man secretive beyond reckoning. I worked with him fifteen years and never found out his age; a drummer and I once jumped him to get his wallet and look at his driver's license, but he brushed us off like roaches. Since all these things intersect, I assume his idiosyncrasies were part of why he could make a bass dance like Ginger Rogers. He had a detailed sense of time you had to work with regularly to grasp, and he taught me, in his subtle way, how immense and elastic a single beat was, that you could play not just in front of it or behind it but around or on top or below, to east or west, inside or outside it.

These two, as tall as their instruments, took it in stride the last few years I played that they would happen to be hanging around out front of the club or bar or restaurant where we were working, no matter how crappy the weather, prepared to open a taxi door and steady me, make sure my cane was solidly planted, give me an arm if I needed it and be diplomatic enough to stay away if I didn't, and shepherd me to the piano where I'd do my damnedest to imitate a functional musician with a painful bone spur. Or any other lame excuse.

Alerted by some telepathy, each man stopped at the hospital the day after my forced return. Afterward they tried calling the apartment but gradually took the hint since I never picked up. Or answered e-mails. Still, those memories of improvising together, concocting something beautiful out of nothing, don't go away no matter how infrequently you meet. To not answer their efforts felt wrong, but writing a book about dying, it turns out, makes you extremely single-minded.

There was another colleague who beat me to the Land of Later On, a burly trumpet player named Herb who'd toured with Parker, with Ellington, with Hampton, with everybody. Having started playing professionally in his early teens, he was a link to a long-lost era, before jazz left the saloons and turned respectable. He'd been my private university, carved the fat out of my playing, told me when I sounded good (originality made him blow you a kiss on the bandstand) and in no uncertain terms when I didn't. He was never scathing, only puzzled, if you didn't hear accurately, but he could always explain how you'd fouled up. He held jazz to the rigorous standards of classical music, and the fact that his chops were going and his range had shrunk to an octave gave me courage as my own skills were waning. He didn't live to hear how bad I got, but he knew what was happening to me even as cancer savaged him faster.

"Don't worry about it, Kip," he'd say. "You'll find over the years that what you lose in technique you gain in musicality. No matter how ragged, we're going to keep making music to the bitter end. And beyond."

I can't convey how depressing it is to know things are only going in one direction, as everything you've worked for all your life is being relentlessly sipped away by some thirsty disease. This was a few years before Lucy got sick, which shrank my own problems to pipsqueak size.

I'd asked about Herb in the afterlife, of course. The wisdom in the clubs was that he'd left word for his wife to await him in their apartment when she showed up. Meanwhile he was visiting sometime before the Civil War, working as the engineer on a locomotive. He'd always believed this was his former incarnation, and now he got to live out the fantasy.

Lucy adored him; we used to have them over for curry dinners one Monday a month, and she and Herb would compete to see who could tolerate more heat. Herb usually won, having briefly been a guest professor at the national conservatory in Kuala Lumpur, though at our regular gig the next night I'd assess the cost of victory in the amount of lip salve he needed.

Long before he admitted he was dying, Lucy guessed. "His taste buds are gone," she said. "I hardly put in any chilies tonight and he couldn't tell."

None of them were with me on that misguided cruise. Herb was already dead; had he been alive he'd have talked me out of it. My excuse (which shivered through me every night on the ship, surrounded by musicians I didn't know) was that when you get unbelievably sick you get unbelievably selfish. Well, Lucy didn't, which was why she had let me go on this fools' voyage. I couldn't even close my eyes and concentrate on the music, because it was really just an aural stimulus to keep the passengers drinking. Plus if I didn't look at the keyboard these days, my fingers might disobey and go anywhere.

Up to now I've been quoting from the guidebook to make my points. I'm going to stop this pretty soon, because though its pages are infested with lies, those lies are also infested with the truth.

The knowledge that loved ones hurt you at a time when nobody knew what other life lay ahead—that they did so thoughtlessly, carelessly, selfishly—is often enough to make you wish never to see them again, no matter what the circumstances of this strange renewed existence.

No wonder she hadn't left word where I should look for her.

THROUGH THE HIMALAYAS

A sojourn in the past provides a chance to test one's patience through slower means of travel. Indeed, some are even drawn to thankfully bygone sensations: the stench of coal-burning trains; the sway, in heavy seas, of a paquebôt; *the exertion of bicycling down sodden lanes and cow paths; the upheaval of trundling in an open car through countryside, klaxoning at sheep.*

Most newcomers find it difficult to reconcile the past with all the expectations one necessarily brings from the future. Condemned to their former present, many decide that enough is enough.

We were standing at a tiny train station among the foothills of the Himalayas, in early morning. The sun was peeping through pine forests; loinclothed sellers of betel-nut and tins of hot curry lunches were ambling along the platform, whose sign read KALKA. British officers, in whiskers and military finery, strode in and out of what was evidently a private waiting room. They took scant notice of us, since we did not merit attention from the Raj.

"The best way to see India," remarked Whitman, "is with Twain. Funny, we detested each other's work before. Now I'd rather be seated next to Sam Clemens in third class, watching him yarn away with scores of untouchables, than in first alongside John Stuart Mill, a much smarter man."

"Will we see him here?"

"Twain? Not a chance. He seldom leaves Hawaii."

"Is he still writing?"

"You could just as aptly ask if he's still breathing."

"I bet he's part of your secret organization, too."

Whitman shook his beefy head. "Tried to corral him. He insisted that what we did was a waste of time. 'Sam,' I answered, 'don't you have plenty of time to waste nowadays? Can you conceive a more fruitful occupation?' He stared at me with that rascally twinkle and said, 'Like preserving the ashes of my cigar? Sorting my waistcoats by date of purchase? Rereading my own books? I can't think of anything *less* fruitful than trying to talk humanity out of anything. You might as well convince a centipede it's wiggling its limbs in the wrong order.'"

There was the approaching hoot of a train.

"Where are we going?" I asked.

I felt I hadn't slept for days; I could still smell the muck of New Guinea, the torment of that Caribbean sugar mill. Our wayward endeavor seemed impossible.

"Simla. Queen of the hill stations. Summer capital of the British Empire in Asia. At this moment it's excruciatingly hot a thousand miles to the south, in Calcutta. So all the officials and their wives, secretaries, servants, paper-wallahs, and sundry hangers-on have decamped up here to think clearly for several months. Like some vast governmental circus."

"Can't we shift ourselves there the usual way?"

"Of course we can," said Whitman. "But I happen to love this little train. I take it whenever the opportunity arises. Doesn't take long—seven hours. I assume Lucy would do the same. So if she's leaving, she'll catch it going back down. Who knows? We might run into her on the Simla platform. Aha."

From a bend emerged a small locomotive pulling three shortened cars.

"Narrow-gauge," said Whitman. "In a century there won't be many left."

The toy train on its toy track chuffed its way to the platform. A gaggle of Indians in uniform scurried importantly over to click open the doors and salute the British officers in. We waited till they were done, then clambered aboard. The officers were seated in the first car, on new leather; a few soldiers and turbaned, cutlassed Sikhs were in the middle car, on what must've been leather once; we were in the third, with natty locals.

"Is there some particular reason we're searching in Simla?"

"You think India's a wild goose chase," said Whitman amiably.

"No, but I hear it's a very big country. Lucy was a yoga teacher. She always talked of visiting historic yoga centers like Mysore. If I'm not mistaken, they're in the south. A long way from the Himalayas."

With a miniature hoot the train lurched off. In third class we settled back against wooden banquettes, having our spines smashed.

"Would you agree that 1878 is not a bad year to start?"

"I have no idea."

The train found its unhurried pace and entered the first of a hundred brief tunnels. We broke out of sooty darkness and back into pine sunlight in seconds.

"The height of the Great Game."

"I don't know what you're talking about."

He lowered his voice beside me, amid the motley noises of the train. "The struggle for control of Central Asia between Britain and Russia, and all the tribesmen whose loyalties they covet. They call it a game, but like the guidebook its instruments are subterfuge, disguise, treason. Murder. And spies of every background and description. Eager ragamuffins from the bazaar. Gnarled old holy men in robes, whose prayer wheels double as encoding machines. French scholars who happen to speak all the languages. Tibetan carpet-traders who turn out to be from Kiev. A colonel's widow from Giggleswick, who chose to stay on and run a boardinghouse for officers whom she entertains most expertly and who thus cannot help but confide in her. Does she realize how very few are deceived? Can she be certain her superiors do not suspect? No one, repeat no one, may be trusted in Simla—where all things begin, and many come to an evil end."

Another tunnel. We started to climb.

"I don't want to be negative, but this really doesn't sound like Lucy's first destination in India."

"You weren't paying attention to her bookshelves," said Whitman mildly. "I can tell you exactly why I found Simla pamphlets in her kitchen drawer."

So now he knew her better than I did.

"Go ahead."

"One of her favorite books—and I say this because I found several copies, including a handsome illustrated edition for which she paid a price that cannot have been negligible—was a novel called *Kim*. By Kipling."

"That's right."

Tunnel after tunnel, though few lasted longer than ten seconds. Each time we came safely out of the cool darkness, everybody smiled in mutual congratulation.

"And did you ever read it?"

"I'm sorry to say I didn't." *Kipling* had been her pet name for me.

"Had you done so, you might have guessed whom we are going to Simla to meet. It would, I admit, be a stroke of extraordinary fortune if Lucy were waiting for us. We have already been lucky and caught her trail in Istanbul. If the laws of temporal gravity were fortuitously organized in the afterlife, we could simply track her down on the afternoons when those two Turkish gentlemen saw her. But those afternoons are gone forever. And that's why we're going to Simla."

"You don't think she's there, you just said so."

I kept being tempted to stick my head out of the window, into the quick night, whenever we burrowed into a stone tunnel. The more tunnels we went through, the more brilliant the sunlight seemed afterward. As the morning advanced and the train struggled its way higher, the heat of the country was left behind.

"No," said Whitman under his breath. "But there's a man we must see, who will be able to tell us if she's still in India. If she passed through, he will know. My guess is she would come to him, because he was immortalized in that wondrous novel. As 'Lurgan Sahib,' shopkeeper of curios. A master of the Great Game."

"I remember her reading me a couple of passages about him."

"It was for such literary fondnesses that I myself visited, years ago. Naturally I wished to learn if there was anybody answering Kipling's description. It turned out the only fiction was his name. If we can persuade him to cooperate, he can help a great deal."

"Suppose she hasn't visited yet?"

"Then," said Whitman, "we are in luck."

"We wait?" Surely he was kidding.

"There are worse places to spend a few years. The air's healthy. There's a marvelous library and fine sweetshops. We're in the decade Kipling wrote about, that Lucy would want to visit. So we're zoning the possibilities efficiently."

"Can't we just ask your friend to keep an eye out and give her a message?"

"You're faltering already," said Walt. "This is the moment, I'm afraid, when everybody, no matter how ardent, loses courage. The size of the past, the size of the world, become overwhelming. To locate anyone seems out of the question."

I didn't answer. The toy train was creeping audaciously up through mists and around folded mountains. Below us lay terraced fields of an extreme green. I stuck my head through the window to enjoy the breeze and get a better look, enjoying the view behind us down the curving tracks. At that instant Whitman yelled, "No!", grabbed the collar of my shirt, and yanked me back. An instant later we dove into another tunnel whose stone wall would've beheaded me.

I collapsed across him in darkness, and as our fellow Indian passengers in the train car chattered away in alarm at my near miss, we pulled ourselves upright on the wooden banquette.

"Boy, that was a close call," I said. "What would that've felt like?"

"Horrible, I would think," said Whitman. As we returned to sunlight he saw I was serious. "More horrible for us than for you. I doubt you'd have felt much."

"So I'd have a headache for a few days? Would I even feel the tunnel wall pass through my forehead?"

He stared at me as if I were crazy.

"Or would my skull get knocked off, and we'd have to stop the train, go back and reattach it?"

He said, "Let me make this very clear. If your head had been severed from your body, you would die."

"I'm already dead."

"Not exactly. You're very much alive in the Land of Later On. Meaning *you*, Kip. If I hadn't saved you—and perhaps a thank-you is in order—you would right now be on the verge of getting born again. As someone else. With absolutely no memory of any of this. Much less of your prior life, with Lucy."

"Born again in the other world? Reincarnated?"

"Bingo."

"That doesn't make any sense, with what you told me."

"I promise you it does."

"You can die here? That's another way of getting people to go back?"

"I'm afraid it is. And against their will, besides. Look both ways the next time you cross Second Avenue."

"Then thank you for saving my . . . life. So when I was attacked in the New Guinea jungle, those men who were shot didn't survive? They were sent back?"

"If their wounds were mortal."

"But why would anyone who's chosen to stay risk it all? And for a war whose outcome is already decided? Does everybody here know this?"

"Of course. But when people stay a long time, they get bored to a degree you cannot imagine yet. They feel immortal, yet their days feel bloodless. They remember wars they fought in the prior life. In youth, when friendships seemed more consequential. They felt afraid, not asleep, and not only each day but each moment mattered. Some admit that they enjoyed having an enemy and trying to kill their enemy. Against all better judgment, they find themselves wanting to revisit that life. It's usually not the ones who were originally killed who want revenge, but the ones who survived for years. And didn't find their comrades when they got here."

"Or couldn't find their loved ones."

"I didn't say that," said Whitman. "I hope you don't feel that." He paused. "Now you understand my perplexity."

THE GREAT GAME AND
ITS MASTER

Assailed by nightmares, I dozed off, and woke whenever we paused at small stations with melodious names. They resembled retirement cottages, surrounded by gardens, in a Victorian England. Cows and water buffalo shambled away at our train; the air became fragrant. As we climbed into afternoon the mountains were obscured by mists. They still did not match my notion of the snowy Himalayas. Whitman jotted in a notepad, murmuring under his breath. Eventually he fell asleep.

Lulled by the altitude and rocked by the slow train, I grew lightheaded. Everything I'd thought all my life, and everything I thought I'd understood since arriving in the afterlife, had turned out to be wrong. I didn't feel dead. I felt fused with my surroundings—the cool air, the spinal discomfort of the wooden seat, the forest vistas and heights of India. But the fellow next to me snoring like a rhino was a poet, my own age, whose work I'd read ninety years after his death; he was taking time out from revising his one book to help find a woman who'd died four years before me; and theoretically I could keep this up as long as I liked, until I tracked her down or got the message she didn't want to see me. Or I could install myself at our apartment and stir up gigs while waiting for former colleagues to show up.

What was strangest was how *normal* this felt, as if I hadn't died to get here. I'd never contracted my disease, and Lucy—similarly brimming with health—was meeting me in Simla, after a vacation in south India on her own, a birthday present I'd bought her. Preferable to think this way, though my flight here had not been a budget air ticket but a bottle from our pharmacy at the corner of 90th and Third.

In my most desperate dreams I'd never believed I might find Lucy waiting in an afterlife. Seated on my bed, that had been a transparent ruse at the last minute to prod myself into slugging down the full container of pills after chipping a tooth prying the thing open. I could no longer play the piano, I couldn't support myself giving lessons, I'd eaten through our careful savings, I was so resentful of what I'd turned into that I stopped seeing beloved friends I'd made music with for decades, I couldn't even stumble across the fucking room without risking a serious fall. There were plenty in much worse circumstances, who'd never enjoyed a tenth of all I had. It'd been a fortunate life, most of the way, I was grateful for that, but I couldn't bear being incapacitated and alone anymore.

Yet here I was, with a second chance whose dimensions were beyond my power to grasp. What I couldn't come to terms with were the faceless forces arrayed to make me give up this richness, this possibility. When immortality gets dropped in your lap the unexpected question is if you can enjoy living with yourself enough to stick around. And the propaganda team broadcasts one message, loud and clear.

We were crossing an arched stone bridge; hawks swung out above a gorge. I watched them dip, and for a moment their flight looked utterly pointless. *Futility*, that was the sensation I felt assaulted by here—a futility immeasurably vaster than the personal version I'd left behind via suicide. It was a feeling I'd struggled against all my life. A determination to learn the piano at any cost had kept me going until I turned into a jaded professional. Then Lucy became my Gibraltar, until her death and my disease. What would I be doing at this moment without Walt beside me? Bouncing off my apartment walls, waiting for a footstep in the corridor that wouldn't ever come? Turning to Billy Boyd for cheeseburgers and solace? Losing all patience, giving in to futility exactly as the guidebook wanted? Going back?

We trundled above the clouds into sunlight burning on Simla, packed precariously across a series of steep ridges. Amid trees rose the sloping roofs and weathervaned spires of bungalows and mansions. I shook Whitman awake.

"Aha," he said groggily. "Hard to believe, isn't it? Several months a year, that's one of the most powerful places on earth."

"Not anymore, surely."

"Oh, there'll always be an England, even in the Land of Later On." He woke up fast. "And an empire. It doesn't exert the muscle it did in my day, but those who choose to act their accustomed roles go through the motions very handsomely, thank you. Nowhere more theatrically than here on Olympus. Paradise of the ruling gods, with their idle wives and spoiled children. Far outnumbered by servants."

On the highest level, where the hill station appeared to stroll even at a distance, stood Simla's emblems: a Gothic church, a town hall, a bandstand, a theater, set on a winding esplanade known as the Mall. Dribbling in profusion below, connected by dizzying staircases and lanes, was a makeshift rabbit warren.

"The lower bazaar," said Whitman acidly. "Would you believe the Brits still refer to it as 'the native quarter'?"

Behind it all was a panorama of hypnotic mountains, finally as snowcapped as they were supposed to be.

The little train reached its station and gave out. No Lucy waiting, of course. We got down last and found that those ahead had grabbed all the human-powered rickshaws, which was fine with me. Walt looked ready to scale the Himalayas.

"We'll take this circuitous path," he said. "Astonishing that there are still people who want to pull more important people around, isn't it?"

It took us twenty minutes, and soon we were lathered in sweat. No one on the Mall was so much as bustling. Men in holiday suits whirled their canes, British women in prim dresses or Indian women in swirling saris twirled parasols, a few officers went clattering by on horseback. Nut-brown monkeys with plaintive faces scampered from rooftop to rooftop and dropped to the dust and gossip below.

"My favorite teahouse," Whitman was saying as we walked. "My favorite coffeehouse. My favorite sweetshop—we'll stop in later. My favorite bookseller. Notice they already carry Kipling's first stories, which will scandalize *le tout Simla*. His novel, though, won't appear until 1901. And here we are. Mr. A. M. Jacob. Curio dealer, magician, orientalist, mystic. A Turk from Isfahan? A Jew from Poland? A Persian, born near Constantinople? Secret agent for Her Imperial Majesty? Or, it is also imputed, Russian spy? A few years from now—in the other life, I mean—he'll be tried, and found innocent, for selling fraudulent jewels. But he'll shut his shop and clear out, fed up but vindicated, his business ruined. He still won't tell me where he went. I'm sure it gives him an enormous satisfaction to stay on, this time around. Meanwhile, we shall determine if Lucy has preceded us."

We had stopped before a dilapidated shopfront on the left, its windows concealed by heavy drapes. A worn sign read: *A. M.*

Jacob Curios. Evidently this was a man able to do business on the strength of reputation alone.

Whitman did not knock, though I would have. With effort he pushed in the massive door and ushered me into a shadow world clogged with fumes. Despite the obvious ease of pulling back drapes to permit sunlight, the shop was only meagerly lit by a few lanterns and smoky candles on tables piled with the debris of Asia. The walls were crowded with masks staring down: howling like devils or grimacing in torment or laughing sardonically or awaiting their opportunity. Hung among them were weapons I'd seen in museums, curved swords and ingenious daggers as well as lances and battle-axes. There was even a full suit of Japanese armor (with a wax figure of a warrior inside it, or maybe it was the fellow himself, preserved) standing in one of the draped windows amid clay water jugs and rolled-up Persian carpets. Antediluvian dust lay on everything, and some masks were being used as hooks for embroidered silks, often in tatters. Gigantic circular trays rusted against the side walls. Several types of joss stick and incense were burning. Elaborate wood or brass tables were crammed obsessively with antique coins, prayer wheels, bizarre and voluptuous oil lamps, books of obscure Eastern religions filled with geometric paintings, beads for counting the names of God, decks of British playing cards, and Buddhas in all postures and sizes, from dourly emaciated to cheerfully obese. There were two wind-up phonographs. On the platter of one was an ear trumpet, on the other a human skull encrusted with silver.

Who was collecting all this stuff in the afterlife? Maybe nobody was.

A sibilant voice whispered from somewhere, "Wal-tair. I am so very glad to see you again. Introduce me to your companion."

I could not locate the disembodied voice.

Whitman pulled me deeper into the gloom. "Kip Sahib, let me present Jacob Sahib, master of the Jewel Game. And other games, besides."

My eyes had grown more accustomed to the dark recesses of the shop, and I realized there was a back alcove, protruding over the sheer hillside and undoubtedly looking down on the lower bazaar. Its windows, too, were thickly curtained to keep out the pestilential daylight. In one corner, from which he could survey any visitor, a slim, black-bearded man was seated in front of a table where he was arranging gems with great patience on a silken thread. He did not look up as he spoke, and it struck me as absurd—or perhaps a deliberate challenge—to not provide himself a candle as he worked. Around his agile hands were piles of jewels and beads like tiny globules; as he bent forward they cast a glow on his face.

He did not put out his hand to either one of us. He said, as if to himself, "And is he a friend of all the world?"

"Not yet," said Whitman.

"Is he come here to be trained by me?"

"We have both come for your help."

"Is he a poet, like yourself?"

"He is a musician. A pianist."

Jacob rummaged through his piles. He glanced at Whitman, then me, as if trying to decide whether we were of any possible use. He inclined his head at a remote province of the shop. "I have had a piano here for three years. A treasure. I acquired it from a brokenhearted maharajah. Your friend ought to look it over."

It was difficult to imagine anyone entering and purchasing a piano. But there were those winking globules of light, strung into a necklace—I could imagine Lucy trying on that sort of treasure.

Whitman said, "What a stroke of luck! A piano."

I took the hint. I picked my way past crates full of straw and poking arms or heads of statuary. Along one wall, buried beneath weavings and bric-a-brac, was a Bechstein upright that might've been dragged by a tractor through a field. I managed to open the lid slightly. All the keys were missing.

"No ivories." I shut it with a bang. "Unplayable."

I wasn't feeling deferential at that moment, especially toward barbarous maharajahs who mistreated superb instruments. Much less their junk dealers.

"So you say," said Jacob mildly. "You are right, I must repair it."

"Don't bother, it's too late. Look, we wanted to ask you—"

"Too late? Surely it is still early afternoon. It is difficult to tell the hour in here, but I find that sunlight muddies the concentration. Only shadows allow my stones to speak with their natural brilliance."

"What I meant," I said, "is that your piano's too far gone. Maybe if it were in Berlin, not the Himalayas, you could get it repaired. The thing's only furniture now. Nobody will ever make music on it again."

"You must not be so hasty. A difficult lesson, I know." To Whitman he added, "How long has he been here? A few hours? This one is a slow learner."

"Not everybody has your patience, Jacob Sahib," said Walt.

"Perhaps you should try the piano again, friend of all the world." He didn't look up, but sifted those long fingers through a pile of jewels. He lifted one stone to within an inch of his forehead and squinted.

"This is ridiculous," I said.

"That is true. It is ridiculous. But you are a friend of Wal-tair, and to me this means you are also a gentleman. So to humor a ridiculous fakir, a dealer in quaint and worthless knickknacks who understands nothing of what is at stake in this life or the last, might you please try that deceased piano once again?"

To move things along I complied. Opened the lid of the dead Bechstein, prepared to shut it instantly.

The full ivory keyboard was there now, flawless. I gulped.

I shouldn't have been surprised, but there are laws of physics I take for granted even in the afterlife. Hastily I moved the dusty fabrics and a couple of engraved lamps to the top of the upright so I could fold back the lid properly. I tried a few experimental chords. Perfectly in tune, with a lovely amenable action. I tried to think if there was something I could play that they'd both recognize, apart from *God Save the Queen*. Ah, the hell with it. I swung into an emphatic blues. Lord, what a piano! After a chorus, still playing, I turned back to the two of them.

"All right, you convinced me—"

Except now there was only Whitman. I stopped.

"He'll appear in a moment. He was trying to prove a point."

"He proved it. Where is he?"

"I have learned," said Whitman gravely, "not to ask."

A brief shimmering, and Jacob was again in front of his work table, rubbing his hands as if from cold. He pulled a tiny sack from a pocket and upended a fresh pile of jewels. He grunted at them. "And is my piano more to your liking?"

"It is, thank you. You'll get a better price now."

"I have no intention of selling it. But I am sure that, because you are an expert, you are right. And now you will in turn, perhaps, be less certain that what is dead must necessarily stay dead."

"I'll keep that in mind." I closed the piano carefully and crossed the shop to rejoin them. "That's why I've come to see you.

I'm looking for a very dear friend. An American woman named Lucy. She read about you—well, someone like you." I described her, and found I was speaking with candor of all she meant to me.

His eyes seemed to glitter, though it may have been the new stones. He heard me out, then said, "She lived here for several months. A discerning customer. She left, she went south, she came back. She seemed genuinely fascinated by India, more than many visitors. I have not seen her for some time."

"You're sure it was her?"

"I am certain that it was she."

"Any idea where she was going?" asked Whitman.

"She found no reason to confide. As you are aware, the bazaars are full of innuendo that I am not what I say I am. A modest dealer in curios and precious stones. All of which, as your discerning friend ascertained, are authentic."

"You and I both know," said Whitman, "that you are not what you say you are. I have seen you float a shattered pot and assemble its pieces in midair without so much as lifting an eyebrow. I have heard your minions report to you, in obscure languages, all the secret goings-on across five frontiers. I have noticed envelopes full of crisp sterling pound notes left in your moldy religious tracts by elderly British ladies, and I have watched you count them. I have observed your eyes illuminated at tiny victories gained in what even the lowliest amahs speak of as the Great Game. And I know you enough, by now, not to believe for an instant any claims of ignorance. Now, please, will you tell us what we need to know?"

Jacob enfolded his fingers in a cat's cradle. He gazed up at both of us and, finally, smiled.

"Very well," he said. "Today is the fifteenth of August. She left Simla on the eleventh of March. She sailed from Calcutta on a merchant ship, eastbound, the morning of the eighteenth. This is reliable knowledge, not hearsay."

"And where was she headed?" I said.

"As I said, she did not enlighten me. She was no more forth-coming than I with her. 'Ask me no questions, I'll tell you no lies,' was a motto she cited, as I recall. Perhaps she wished to demon-strate that she was more adept than I."

"So how can I find out?"

"I expect that you might make inquiries in Calcutta at the ticket offices, and learn that way. Or, if you are prepared to be patient, I shall make inquiries for you. But I do not have such information."

"Jacob Sahib, I don't believe you," said Whitman.

The curio dealer sighed. "This is the constant penalty of wis-dom. No one trusts what you say."

"Not if they know you."

"As you prefer." He stared, piercingly, straight at me. "And indeed, I was lying. She is en route for the Pacific. To the Marquesas Islands. The slow method. If you hurry, you may catch her."

A MORE SERIOUS
MISSTEP

For those first hours home after my March jazz cruise I didn't want to accept that Lucy's world would even on good days be bounded by a few blocks around our apartment, she was now too weak to travel. I hastily offered to buy her a wheelchair and put together the trip I'd promised, to the dramatic landscapes of the Southwest she recalled fondly from a childhood expedition. Surely, I argued, once we left there was nothing for us to hurry back here to do, we had plenty of time.

We were sitting beside each other on our weary sofa. I'd helped her out of bed, brewed a pot of her favorite herbal tea.

"*You* have plenty of time," she said. "I don't. Perhaps we could've even gone away last month, if we were both less blindly optimistic. You and I weren't ever any good at doing things at the right moment, were we? We should have made our trip right after my diagnosis."

"It was winter. We'd never get our covered wagons through the snowdrifts."

"You'd have been stronger then, also. The doctors are too cowardly to spell out you're never, never, never going to be as healthy as you are that very morning. And you'd better take advantage of it. You have to hold them over a fire to get them to tell you ten percent of the truth."

"It's against their fucking hypocritic oath."

As if by getting angry alongside her, I could transfer responsibility from my shoulders to the medical profession's.

"Listen to you swear, Twinkletoes," she said gently. "You should've heard the goddamned nonsense I shot off the walls while you were away on your floating gig. Our diseases have made us furious at the world in ways we never were before. They've taught us nothing."

"Well, it's not an education we chose."

"It's still an education. Pretty soon I get to graduate. But what good is a posthumous diploma? They'll find a way to hit you with my bill, just wait."

"Lucy, stop."

"Don't pay it. They give up eventually. Everyone does."

What was that supposed to mean?

"A half year from now," she went on, "maybe even by midsummer, I'll be dead. Then you'll be stuck here alone with a different set of problems. You know, I wouldn't resent it if you found some lovely young thing to look after you. Actually, I kind of like the idea."

"I don't want to have this conversation."

"We need to have this conversation. Not that I'll be gazing down at you through a telescope from some cloud. Or watching on some eternal television screen. You can fool around all you want without looking over your shoulder. Go ahead, knock yourself out."

She seemed to be enjoying herself.

"Lucy, this is pointless."

"As Billy says, the chicks love a great piano player."

"Like he's an expert. Besides"—I nudged her—"I'm not a piano player anymore. I'm only a struggling piano teacher without a fancy degree. Remember how disdainful you were when we met? As if I were a criminal, hoodwinking my students into enjoying music."

"That was an icebreaker."

"Sounded pretty sincere to me."

"Then I guess it worked, didn't it?"

We didn't speak for a moment. It was dinnertime, but the plan I'd nurtured since morning, on my three planes from Florida (saving the cruise line forty bucks), would have to be abandoned. No way Lucy had the strength to go to a restaurant.

She said quietly, "While you were gone all I could think about was how we gave up the trip we always talked about. So you could make a thousand dollars playing with musicians you don't even respect. And fool yourself that your career isn't over. You know it, your colleagues know it, it's just a question of when you have the courage to stop once and for all. No matter what kind of offer you get to embarrass yourself for decent money. That's the truth, Kip. This is why we're together, to tell each other what other people won't. "

"I'm so sorry," I managed. "Getting sick has made me selfish."

"Bullshit. Doing something well made you selfish."

"I do realize," I said, "it was a mistake to do the cruise. But neither of us expected you to be like this three weeks later. I wish there were some way to wind the time back, but there isn't. We have to hope you get a little better as the weather gets better. Then we seize our opportunity."

"What opportunity?"

"We can leave in a day. Nothing to cancel. We'll take off. Don't worry, I've learned my lesson. No force on earth would make me play another gig. I do have some self-respect left. Even if I don't deserve yours anymore."

"Stop talking crap," she said. "Do you think my respect for you is so vulnerable? That my love gives up so easily?"

"I'd understand if you did."

She shrugged beside me, and laid her head on my shoulder; I can still feel its particular weight all these years later, still smell her that evening, along with a faint frightening odor of illness. "It's just another experience we won't get to share. There are too many, and that trip is easy to point at. We never got to be parents either. And years from now, because I know you're going to live a long time, you're going to live out the decades for both of us no matter how sick you become, Kip, I want you to keep imagining the alternate life we didn't get to share. I want you to imagine it in extraordinary detail. For both of us. I want everything to go our way in your imagination. I want miracle cures, I want plenty of success, I want oodles of journeys. Feel free to invent me a time machine, too. Make sure we live forever while you're at it."

IN THE MARQUESAS

"I only met Melville once," Walt was saying. "In lower Manhattan."

We stood at the highest point of Nuku Hiva. I looked past forested spears and crags, across disordered slopes, to a blue Pacific. Valleys rose in a delirium of palms to pillars of rock, like spires of some surreal cathedral. I don't believe in prayer, but this was a beauty I could see praying to, and Lucy would've had the same reaction. What would she have said? *Of all the places I have ever been, this is where I most would want you to find me.* I closed my eyes to feel her beside me, until Walt started up again.

"It was a few years after the war of secession. His white whale had already been harpooned by the public. A quarter-century had passed him by since his big best seller about jumping ship to live among cannibals on this very island. He struck me as a ruined man. Thwarted by perpetual solitude in the heart of the population. Haunted by the rare opportunity to earn a fee from lecturing on those exploits. All anyone wanted to hear about was his fragrant nude Fayaway. Might she yet be found on Nuku Hiva? Did she have any lovely younger sisters?"

We were gazing down on the broad horseshoe bay of the only town in the Marquesas. Large enough, as Whitman said, to have a post office and a jail, though prisoners were given keys. I assumed it was the present; the copra freighter roped to the harbor quay seemed contemporary. It was dizzying to arrive so effortlessly.

So this had once been Melville's place. Technically, it always was, since we—or Lucy—could travel back two centuries to his era whenever we wanted.

"I told him how much I admired his whale, that I thought it the best English prose of our age. I doubt he recognized my name. He stared at me like a drunkard from a fever-dream, swallowed, and intoned, 'Keep true to the dreams of thy youth.' That was all I got out of him, poor fellow. I had hopes for a friendship."

"He gave up on the afterlife, I assume."

"Lost both his sons long before his own time. One a suicide, by pistol and ball. The other a vagabond *isolato* like himself, who went to sea. They weren't waiting when he arrived, so he tried it for only a weekend. I didn't learn he'd gone back until it was too late. If I could've persuaded Melville to visit this part of the world as he knew it, he might be with us yet. He thought humanity would've been better off had Polynesians been the missionaries, rather than their victims. Once again, a particular man is gone forever. Not to mention the books he might've written, relieved from a thousand daily irritations that nibble away the soul."

Having been here so long, Whitman spoke of the Land of Later On without irony, as one's real existence. And the prior world as an unfortunate alternative.

Pointing to the prodigious view, he added gently, "If you ask me, anyone who is tired of islands is tired of life."

"We should've asked your jeweler friend which island Lucy was headed for."

"Kip, she wasn't on that freighter. It's the only vessel that regularly visits the Marquesas. We'd have seen her disembark. Never mind, it's back in four weeks."

As if we had all the time in the world to hang around.

"She could've been on it last month. Maybe she got off before Nuku Hiva."

Walt looked pained. "If it's Melville she's after, she's certain to come here. There was that pamphlet in her kitchen drawer. And before she hurries back to the bloodthirsty Taipivai valley, 1842, I reckon she'll explore the present. If she has the slightest bit of sense, anyway. Melville's Taipivai was hardly a stroll in Kipling's Simla. Although, by the by, women could take as many husbands as they liked."

Multiple husbands? Was this meant to reassure me? The slightest bit of sense? That wasn't Lucy. I imagined her darting fearlessly around the past, game to witness anything, even a cannibal feast.

It bugged me that we hadn't met her 1878 sailing ship from Calcutta at any Eastern ports. There were plenty of routes then as far as Tahiti, but only this one reliable modern freighter from there to here if she was determined not to cheat by jumping, and sample the island's present before exploring its past.

"Whenever you search for someone in the afterlife, Kip—can you manage a hike?—you wait at their ultimate destination. Then you rummage around week to week in hopes they're rummaging as well. It never pays to bottleneck their approach from different locales. The forking paths are too numerous, too divergent."

Typee had been her favorite Melville work ever since college. She'd given me a copy soon after we met, in that period when to share books is a shorthand for explaining yourself. I felt a bit jealous of the young sailor, not for his escapades (Fayaway unwraps her only garment to use for a sail—as Walt said, "establishing

South Seas tourism in one billowing sentence") but because I saw how strongly Lucy was attracted to somebody capable of deserting ship.

Fleeing civilization was a deep fantasy in her. She used to talk of whether it might be feasible to live alone on a tropical island for a year. I realized the smart move was to go along with the idea, discussing the details, making it clear I'd miss her yet never stand in her way. Soon enough her plan would get shoved to the back of the atlas. She never used it as a threat, but held on to the dream unventured.

"I still think we should speak to the freighter's crew," I told Whitman. "Ask if they've seen her. Warn them to be on the lookout."

Whitman said, "No point, Kip. The crew are Tahitian or Marquesan. Even the captain and supercargo are from the Tuamotus. They simply won't recall who was aboard the last voyage. Or think to give her a note three voyages hence. She might decide en route to spend a few months in Bali or Macao. In which century? There's no use trying to anticipate such impulses. A sobering thought, I'm afraid."

At that moment I'd had too much to drink, in a short time, of his sobriety.

"So now what?"

"The only thing we can do is hike into the Taipivai valley. If she's not there we'll wait a month. I have a friend who showed me around some years back. He'll be a big help. He'll have seen her, in one century or another."

Walt seemed to have been everywhere, to always have local friends.

This high up there was plenty of breeze. As we began to descend along a steep rough road, the air grew close. The valley opened like a rib cage of palms, with a river meandering thinly past a village before widening to a bay. Inland, a makeshift track sliced across the ribs and wound tortuously into dense wilderness. At the valley's head, two slender waterfalls hung down from mountains and clouds.

"Now we're in the valley of the Taipis. According to Melville, he spent four months as their prisoner. I suspect it was four weeks, and very friendly. But a young writer should be excused for embroidering his memories. Ah, here's Falchetto."

At the edge of the village, lined with banana, mango, and frangipani trees, waited a light-skinned, solid man in his sixties with a wooden cross dangling at his neck and a face of rugged vivacity. He seemed to have observed us from afar. When he recognized Whitman he hurried to greet us with a headlong schoolboy gait. I mistook Falchetto for a missionary gone native, and Walt told me later that the man had visions. He spoke a garbled French which, despite the afterlife's crash course, I barely understood.

They shook hands and kissed each other's cheeks before I was introduced.

"Falchetto was born and raised in Taipivai," said Whitman. "His father's lungs were damaged in World War I, so he came out to keep bees and recover. Falchetto knows every path in this valley. The Melville scholars never interview him, but then they'd rather not discover how much of *Typee* was truth, not fable."

I delicately reminded Whitman why we were here.

"Yes, yes, of course." In Istanbul I'd seen Walt adopt minor Turkish gestures, arching his eyebrows, tilting his head. Now he gesticulated, recounting in theatrical French all he knew of my life story, the piano, my disease and suicide, finally Lucy.

Falchetto patiently let him finish, then announced, "She's here."

I saw nobody around us. A hillside of palms swept back from a blue wooden church with a rusted roof.

"Are you certain?" asked Whitman.

"She has been here a month. *Une Americaine*. I took her to see the temple *marae*, with the statues, that your friend Belleville wrote about seeing at the end of his visit. She went for her hike up the valley this morning. We can find her, or wait until she comes back. She's staying at the house of my eldest daughter."

"We're in luck," said Walt, translating. "Would you like to wait for her?"

"What planet are you on?" I nearly yelled.

It seemed unbelievable: everything I'd just seen, she'd just seen.

"I beg your pardon?"

"Let's find her right away."

In Manhattan and by the Bosphorus I'd been years behind. In Simla her trail felt warm, but to miss someone in the afterlife by months might mean continents and centuries. Yet Lucy was at that very instant a few miles away, in this sequestered valley of palms near the waterfalls Melville had described. Waiting for me to find her.

Fired by the search, Falchetto ran us ragged. Barefoot, he scrambled through the thick hillside, clambering over muscular vegetation with such agility that Walt and I couldn't keep up.

We found him waiting in clouds of mosquitoes that he apparently didn't notice, where the ground leveled to a path winding through trees, an ancient road of rocks. Just below, following the trickling river for miles, were house foundations—boulders the size of a small car, moved down from the cliffs and fitted into place without benefit of the wheel—the ruins of the Taipi tribe, Walt explained, whose last gasp Melville glimpsed before European diseases all but obliterated them.

"Death," Whitman muttered, "coming in like a tide."

No signs of Lucy, nor could I see through the foliage to the waterfalls that I heard ever louder. Almost imperceptibly, the path was rising.

"I showed her this path the second morning she was here," said Falchetto proudly. "Now she knows it as well as I do. Maybe we'll never find her!"

Our search for Lucy had made her a kind of celebrity.

I remembered one of our first dates—she'd suggested we meet at a flea market on a Sunday morning. Could we locate each other amid the scrimmage of Manhattanites hunting for deals? I came up behind her without calling her name. Somehow she knew I was there, and turned with perfect timing to embrace me.

"Does she stay here on her walks?" I asked, out of breath. "Or does she go back a century or two?"

"No, no," Falchetto scoffed. "At first, yes. She asked if it was safe. So I took her myself, I introduced her to my great-great grandfather *maternel*, who gave his word to look after her. He was a chief, you know. She told me she went back a few times but preferred the solitude of today. You think this is solitude? I told her. Wait till you see Taipivai a hundred years from now. When nobody lives here."

What do you do, alone every day? I wondered. What do you think about? All the years with me? The years without me?

"I wonder what she does to occupy herself," said Walt absently, in French, to Falchetto. Often I felt him trying to disguise the fact that he had his finger on the pulse of my thoughts. My French was improving by the minute.

"She draws pictures," said Falchetto, "with colored pencils. I think we must try the temple *marae*. If she were on this path she would have heard us coming."

A new hobby of hers. It was a relief to hear she was always alone. Nobody ever said: Yes, she was with a handsome man, they must be very much in love.

We'd been climbing steadily up the valley slope, the wilderness more austere. We could see both waterfalls. It was hard slogging and even Falchetto, who talked under his breath in some Marquesan dialect, fell silent.

Then, without warning, we came to an open glade with twelve mossy statues of obese men clutching their bellies, phalli dangling, beside women with great breasts and welcoming bodies. I was ahead of Whitman and Falchetto—their eyes were on the sacred sculptures, mine on a patch of white in trees at the edge of the glade. I knew that blouse; I'd bought it for her during our first trip together, with money that tourists left in the brandy snifter on the hotel piano each night.

"Lucy!" I shouted immediately. "Lucy, it's me!"

Time is deceptive: I was too slow. She turned for a lengthy instant toward me. I saw her face, fully lit by a streak of sunlight, but as I was coming out of obscuring shadows, she may not have seen mine. No, she'd definitely recognized me—our moment of staring across the glade at each other was too long for her not to have. But that was too awful to accept. My mouth was open when her white blouse vanished, and she disappeared into the afterlife's gaping abyss.

YOUR FRIEND, WALT WHITMAN

We stayed in Taipivai a couple of nights, sleeping at Falchetto's, in case Lucy decided to come back. I couldn't summon the slightest belief that she would. She'd left nothing at the cottage of Falchetto's daughter, who was not surprised ("Well, what is there to do here but stay or leave?" she said with a smile) but offered me Lucy's sketch pad with a few local scenes. I handed it back; Lucy hated saying good-bye, and the colored drawings would've been her modest thank-you.

I tried to convince myself she hadn't recognized me. Clearly she had. I couldn't avoid something she'd said a month after I returned from that jazz cruise, after I'd theoretically been forgiven. We were talking of whether your attitude changed once you knew your days were numbered. Surely, I said, this made life more precious? She shook her tousled head. "You think your love for the world is boundless, then you realize that it's not at all. There are boundaries to everything."

I had felt she was talking about us. It was impossible, now, not to lose heart.

To keep me quiet, Walt gave the freighter's crew a brief letter I wrote her, in case she boarded from other Marquesan islands. A day later the ship moved on.

My vote was to return to New York and wait at the apartment, as in my note.

"You're surrendering," said Whitman. "You mustn't lose faith so easily. Impossible to imagine coming any closer than we have. You're right on her trail, you're an inch from her thoughts, you're practically within her heart."

"Closer? She could be anywhere."

She'd stared straight at me. I felt certain she was fleeing me.

"*'I cannot be awake, for nothing looks to me as it did before,'*" said Walt. He had a habit of quoting his own poetry. "*'Or else I am awake for the first time, and all before has been a mean sleep.'*"

"You don't think I'm going to succeed, do you."

He sighed. "I know the chaos around you feels total. Yet all this disorder is fol-de-rol, an illusion. No one knows her as you do. No one else can imagine where she might go next. The afterlife is a thick-skinned beast, you have to keep whacking away at its hide. For all you know, she's also looking for *you*. Ever think of that?"

"Then we're both doing a clumsy job."

"You mustn't give up trying to see your way feelingly into who she is. You say you don't know where to find her? Not so. She's standing just behind you."

"None of this," I said, "does me any good."

"I warned you it could be this way. All right, we'll go back to New York. But let's stop elsewhere en route. Not for long. Humor me. A favorite place of mine, for personal reasons. There's something I want to talk to you about."

His hand at my elbow, we jumped from wet Polynesian sunlight to a dry hot night of stars. We were walking by an American highway. Every now and then a gigantic truck, lit up like an ocean liner, roared past in the opposite direction. Walt would raise his hand in greeting at the headlights—his eyes mild, his gait loping.

Ahead was the neon sign of a truck stop, a faint orange smudge on darkness.

"I don't think you give me enough credit," he said, "for living in the future. My future, I mean. It probably strikes you as more convenient. Better plumbing. No cholera epidemics. Ballpoint pens. Right?"

"Something like that." Not that I'd mulled what drove him. I knew without Walt I wouldn't have gotten far, and confirming that Lucy was still in the Land of Later On was enormous. It hadn't crossed my mind that there might be a favor he wanted me to do for him, or his secret organization, in return.

We traipsed toward the glow a half mile away.

"But I have my private reasons," Whitman continued. "Early on, I vowed to think for myself and avoid the fashions of my era. The problem was, my motivation depended on the truism that we're going to die. Near the end of my life I put out what I called the Deathbed Edition of my book. It never occurred to me I might also one day toss that version down the air shaft, and begin revising anew. After you get here, it changes the meaning of perfection. I'm sure, as a musician, you understand."

"Sorry, but there's no perfect performance of Beethoven. There sure as hell isn't a perfect improvised version of some Ellington tune. That's why we live to fight another day. Besides, music always vanishes, that's what music is."

Whitman trudged ahead in silence, while I thought irritably: Why are we wasting our time on this highway? You don't think Lucy's sitting alone in a booth up ahead, lingering over a milkshake?

Surely what I'd glimpsed in Taipivai was not Lucy going back permanently, but shifting elsewhere to elude me. Escaping.

"Nevertheless," he said, "I thought that if I worked hard enough, experimented long enough, I'd become a perfect writer.

Who could make words sing, dance, kiss. Bear children. Weep, bleed, stab, steal. Sack cities. Steer ships. Charge with cavalry. Do anything a man or woman can. Unfold into friendship or love. But my determination was based on knowing I'd die."

I did see his point: all my focus on music had unconsciously sprung from knowing my time on earth was limited. Once the piano was gone, once Lucy was gone, death efficiently made up my mind. I couldn't find a single reason not to hurry toward it. Only an idiot waits for a miracle cure, and I could no longer extract satisfaction from anything. Not even some recording I'd always loved.

I said, "Lucy and I knew one of us would die first, but at least we'd be happy for years and years. We were so sure of that."

I omitted the rage, which ultimately required more energy than the disease left me, and was none of his business.

"And what," asked Walt tenderly, "have you learned since coming here?"

Ahead was the truck stop, lit up as if it were the Ritz. *The Jukebox Joint*, said the orange neon, and below that in blue: *Groovy Music, Groovy People.*

"I should've killed myself right after Lucy died. Then I'd have found her."

"Perhaps," said Whitman. "Perhaps not."

A dozen cars and a couple of rigs were pulled off the highway at the sign.

"It's no wonder," he added, "that so many people turn tail and go back." Onto his agenda again. "Like a fellow who wins the lottery, then does his best to spend his unfathomable wealth quickly. Nothing prepared him for it, he doesn't recognize himself. He'll do anything to return to a world he knew. People construct their lives around a fiction they're going to die. In one fell swoop they're here, and learn they can stay as long as they like. Not an inch of it resembles any afterlife they conceived of. Soon they realize they don't care for eternity. Once you grasp that you can go everywhere, you no longer want to go anywhere."

"I still don't understand why you and your colleagues try persuading people. There are too many. Like grains of sand on a beach. Why bother?"

"You have to start somewhere. Less useless than rewriting the same book. It's a sociable way to spend one's time. After all, no matter what happens, we're friends, aren't we?"

No matter what happens struck terror in my gut. For some time I'd been troubled that Walt knew much more of what lay ahead than he was telling.

I said, "But if you and your cabal succeed, you'll remove lots of potentially special people from the world. The other world, I mean."

We'd reached the truck stop, a low concrete building with long windows by the parking lot. It droned with multiple air conditioning units. The neon sign was buzzing like a cicada. This sweaty Oklahoma night was hotter than the Marquesas.

"The other world," said Whitman dryly, "can shell its own peas."

He pulled open the glass door. A bar, an illuminated jukebox, formica tables, blue vinyl booths. Mostly men drinking, a few couples. A country song was quietly playing, the usual wit and heartbreak set to six twanging chords. Luckily the place was as cold as a meat locker. Walt ordered us beers and we sat down in a booth.

"You've been here before?"

"Several times," said Walt. "Though my reputation was for not ever liking anyone else's poetry, I'm a fan of Hank Williams. I like the jukebox selection, I like watching people listen. And, I must admit, I got lucky here."

Meaning—?

"Oh, a trucker. Who plowed through a guardrail. Missing his wife and kids, who might not join him for an awfully long time. Like me, someone of both persuasions. Never saw him again, so I guess I wasn't persuasive. Still, those who love each other shall be invincible, no matter how little apparently remains of their love. It is the joy we remember that is immortal. You see? That's a perspective whose veracity only death can prove."

I didn't want to hear this perspective. I also didn't want to know about his personal life. He'd been here a hundred twenty years longer than I, but evidently still had passions. I wondered how long Lucy's patience for solitude had lasted.

"You're shocked," he added, "at my romantic confession."

I saw he would've liked me to be. "Not at all."

He inclined his buffalo head. "You know, my other life was a cavalcade of such disappointments. In the war I gave my heart—even some not-so-chaste kisses—to several young soldiers who either died of their wounds or went back after the hostilities to their families. There was a Tom, and an Elijah. There was even the wife of a friend. There were others. Had I been caught younger I might've married, but I saw to it I was not. I used to envy them their children, if not their permanent linkages. After the war there was a paroled rebel soldier twenty-eight years younger than I. Closer to me than any of them, but Peter did not realize all I was offering until it was too late. Age, alas, settles many questions."

"And you never found them here?"

"Never. Not one. This is what awakened me to the problem at hand. So that I became, as it were, a ringleader. My biographers like to say I needed my life to be incomplete so my work could fully absorb me, but this makes me sound even more egotistical than I was. The right person could've—look at that!"

A ballad had started on the jukebox. Several couples stood to dance, and not eight bars into the song they were airborne together, just as at Nôtre Dame. Even the gents at the bar, clutching their drinks like lead weights, drifted off their stools.

All of us in booths stayed down; the tables kept bumping us to the floor.

"I never tire of seeing this," said Whitman. "Anyway, as you so aptly point out, the problem is too vast. Grains of sand, indeed. And no practicable way to circumvent the guidebook. Nobody ever used publication to his own ends more strategically than I, except the Church. But here the game is rigged, and there's no getting around it. The only solution would be to beat them to the punch."

"I don't understand."

I felt Walt's dismay, but it made my heart lift to see music floating people off the ground. Like a soaring vindication of every belief I'd staked my life on.

"Get 'em before the guidebook does. Before they're even dead."

FINDING LUCY

There is an unexplainable gravitational pull between some people, a forceful tug of loyalty and affection that Walt called "adhesiveness." I don't think anyone would dispute that it exists, and goes beyond links of background, culture, language. Or era, in the Land of Later On.

I got all the reminder I needed at that Oklahoma truck stop when, as we sat talking in our booth, I noticed Whitman kept glancing over my shoulder at the bar. As he normally fixed you right in the eye, even stared you down, I turned during a jukebox break in the love songs, once everybody floated back to the floor—and saw he was exchanging meaningful gazes with a bearded fellow who'd come in.

"You know," I said, "I think I'll head back to New York and gather my wits. Billy may have a useful idea or two. I can track you down at Lucy's studio."

"Seems sensible," said Walt.

"I don't want to cramp your style."

That made him grin. "Nobody has ever cramped *my* style."

But this wasn't true—he was a man ruled by loneliness and yearning. He was their master only when he was writing.

I stood up. "I assume I won't end up in the New Guinea jungle this time."

"Not a chance. You're an experienced shifter now. The trick is staying focused. Don't let any stray thoughts get the better of you. Especially, don't get distracted from when and where you're going."

They omit these handy tips from the guidebook, naturally.

I went from the truck stop into the overheated night. Beyond the civilizing glow of the neon sign, the stars were out in their far-flung allegiances—they would be invisible over a lit-up Manhattan. Walt must already be proving his theory of adhesiveness. More power to him, I thought. Wondering what lay ahead, I jumped.

That was my mistake: thinking about the future. I blinked at harsh noon sun. I was standing outside my brownstone on 88th, but it wasn't a version I knew of my street. The buildings had been sandblasted, as if scraped by light. Pavements were absolutely spotless. People dressed either more streamlined or more eccentrically. The air smelled different, too—what was it? Oh, right. No cars.

If this was the future, it wasn't far off. Three decades? At least I'd got the right address. Better than being shot at in some swamp; maybe I'd stumble on a clue.

The first thing I did was hurry up the steps. No name on my mailbox. I buzzed, but whoever was living there didn't buzz back. I was going to try the key in my pocket, but the lock was gone. Instead there was an electronic-eye device whose slot refused to acknowledge my fingerprints. So that was that.

I examined the other mailboxes. I didn't recognize any names, but people might easily move away. I did notice that Billy Boyd's annoying nephew Norm had taken over his apartment, as in the prior life. He'd be in his fifties now, or perhaps he'd elected to remain in his twenties forever. Death by mouthwash, probably. He was Billy's opposite, having been raised specifically not to turn out like his wicked uncle. The sort of well-meaning twerp who cleans his nails several times a day.

In the last year of my life he'd moved in after Billy lost to stomach cancer and no other relatives wanted the lease. Our first disagreement came when he boasted that he'd boxed Billy's manuscripts on the sidewalk for the garbage men to take away; he wanted me to congratulate him on his antiseptic taste. Beyond that, he was constantly offering to lend a hand—which, when you're trying to pluck up the courage to commit suicide, is a form of aggression. After countless bacon cheeseburgers together, for me Billy's sallow, unshaven countenance represented human beauty, while his nephew's pristine cheeks were a disavowal of the family reprobate. I always feel that art springs more from dirt than from fine intentions: given the choice, I put my trust in dirt.

I went back to the street and headed left, up to Third.

I had no particular goal. Upper Manhattan as a pedestrians-only zone had to be experienced to be believed. Third Avenue, gussied up during my two decades, was now a lavish boulevard. Money had sluiced in from somewhere after my death, carrying away the poorer flotsam on a powerful current. But what was I thinking? This wasn't the city's actual future, only a stage set. No one here had to put up with rent spikes. Or suffer a debilitating illness. Or early extinction, unless they chose to abandon the Land of Later On.

No thank you, I thought. *I'm* not going back, whether or not I locate Lucy.

I started walking up Third Avenue out of a kind of archaeological curiosity, wondering which establishments had survived. The locksmith was gone, both our Chinese restaurants were gone (replaced by art galleries, since everyone in the afterlife was an eager amateur), and a thrift store where they'd known us by name was now a French bistro. Midday was brighter than I recalled—the light changes in cities every generation—but I couldn't tell which buildings had been torn down.

No, there was one holdout. A pharmacy: there must be a postmortem need for aspirin. Or rarefied teas, since this place was owned by a Bangalore gentleman who imported herbal concoctions before all the supermarkets stocked them. (Lucy was a top customer.) Everyone loved buying their prescriptions from Mr. Mistry, and he'd destroyed all competitors by naming his drugstore the "House of Mistry."

Perhaps he was still here, ageless in a white smock, happy to chitchat with ageless clientele. Or perhaps his son had taken over the role. I crossed the avenue to pay my respects; for years they'd furnished me with drugs that did no good, the best medical science had to offer. And that was when I saw Lucy, stepping into the sunlight, pulling the pharmacy door behind her, a small paper bag in one hand.

I wasn't going to lose my chance at her again.

"Lucy!"

She still had a Marquesan tan, the flush of months journeying on a slow 19th century ship from Calcutta to the Pacific islands. And the glow of a year outdoors, some of it barefoot. I put her in her early thirties. She appeared as fully herself as I remembered. That upright lovely posture, so unwavering.

"Lucy! It's me! Over here!"

Had she gone deaf? She was glancing around to see who was being yelled at. Not responding to her own name. Something was definitely wrong.

I was a few steps away when she finally noticed me hurrying toward her. She gave a faint smile, right into my eyes, but it wasn't a smile that knew me. Her confusion pulled me up short on the sidewalk. At least she hadn't vanished yet.

"Lucy," I said gently, resisting the urge to take her in my arms, "it's me, Kip. I've been searching all over for you. All over."

Her eyes were kind. "I'm sorry. My name's Suzy."

Every inch of her was unmistakably the person I knew.

I swallowed. "Well, I think your name is Lucy."

"Well, I think that since you seem to know what everybody's name is better than they know themselves, maybe you should walk into this pharmacy and take a number and ask to get your head examined." She smiled sweetly.

This was definitely Lucy. Where was Walt Whitman when you needed him?

"You don't remember me, do you. Your name is Lucy Crandall. I've been looking for you all over the world. All over the past." I was jabbering, in case she didn't let me finish. "In Istanbul. In Simla. Just a few days ago, in the Marquesas. You looked right at me. We shared an apartment a couple of blocks from here for eighteen years. I play the piano. You died of leukemia four years before I did—"

"So you've been following me. How am I supposed to feel about that?"

No wonder she hadn't recognized me on Nuku Hiva, when I called her name.

"You're not saying you caught leukemia from me, are you?" she went on.

"No, I had my own disease for years, I couldn't play the piano anymore. After you died I lost hope. Eventually I decided to kill myself. Best decision I ever made. I've been searching for you ever since I got here."

"I can't imagine," she said quizzically, "living with someone suicidal."

Was this an act? It couldn't be. I felt I was going out of my mind.

"Don't you remember your studio down on Duane Street? That's where we fell in love. Back in 1987. You kept a photo of me on your desk, from the first trip we took together. I was leaning against a coconut palm."

"Boy, you really *have* been following me. How did you know to go there? I haven't visited that place in ages."

Maybe she'd blanked me out as a way of getting rid of what I'd done, what I failed to do, a few months before her death.

She gazed at me askance. "I guess it could've been your picture. I wasn't sure that was my studio. I did go there. All the books had somebody else's name in them."

It was dawning on me that she truly didn't have the faintest idea who she was. How had Walt referred to it? "Drinking from the waters of Lethe en route." She was dressed like her old self, however—a green silk blouse and fetching '50s tap dancer shorts, as she called them. I always wonder if women fully appreciate that, by standing in place and staring you in the eye, they can skitter whatever gyroscope you possess.

"Anyway, how did you know to follow me to all those places?"

"Don't you see? I knew where you would go. I'm telling you, I know you, Lucy." I wasn't convincing her, I could see, but she wasn't calling the cops either. "There were all those pamphlets in your kitchen drawer, too."

"So it wasn't a partner's insight," she said. "It was pamphlets."

I stood there exasperated, at a loss for what approach to take. No matter what, I'd come across as a stalker.

I said, "Okay. If your name's not Lucy, tell me why you think it's Suzy."

"Because that's what the person called me when I arrived. And she seemed to know me."

"Who was she?"

"Why should I tell you? You'll just say she was wrong, and you know me much better." But there was doubt in her voice, at last.

"I promise I won't say that."

I was wondering, still, why the person who met me off the ferry hadn't been Lucy, but Dr. McMillan.

"If you must know, though I'm not sure why I'm telling you, it was an elderly Dutch woman."

"You're telling me because, down deep, you trust me implicitly. You know who I am, even if you can't put it into words." It took great self-control not to sweep her off her feet—as I hadn't been able to for years, thanks to my disability. "I bet I can tell you where, too. Where you emerged after dying." At this point I knew her life story immeasurably better than she did. "It was southern California, wasn't it? At a yoga retreat. And the elderly Dutch woman was your teacher. Her name was Ingrid. She was the person you trusted most before you met me. You know as much as I do that something built into the mechanism here reaches into your unconscious and finds whoever's dead that you consider totally trustworthy to greet you when you arrive. And explain things. This woman was your first serious yoga teacher. Which was your profession, though you may not remember. You told me the story of attending this retreat many times. How you felt a profound bond even though she never got your name right and died before you could study with her again. It didn't matter, you had absolute confidence in everything she said."

My speech had taken Lucy aback. I saw that no matter how little of it she consciously knew, every word rang solidly.

"In that case," she said quietly, "if we lived with each other all those years, why wasn't I the one who met *you*? You didn't trust *me*, it seems."

No, the other way round.

"Maybe because you don't realize who you are. How should I know?"

Argumentative to the end, she said, "You're the person with all the answers. I can't help it if I ask a few obvious questions."

"Let's try to convince you. I'll tell you what you've got in that paper bag."

"Go ahead."

"In fact, I bet you once had a similar conversation with Mr. Mistry about your name. The first time you walked in there. He called you *Lucy*. Am I right?"

"This time you're wrong, Kip. Wasn't that your name? There is no Mr. Mistry. Don't let me interrupt, you were about to clairvoyantly tell me what I bought."

I put my hand out gently, making fun of myself as a mind reader by touching my fingers to her forehead. She took a quick step back—I wasn't doing remotely as well as I imagined. "Sorry."

"Look, either you know, or you don't."

What did it take to convince her? She wouldn't have been standing on the sidewalk had she not spent four years doubting her name, aswirl in questions about who she'd been, how she'd gotten here. Had she not sensed secretly that I was, in her former life, who I said I was. It spoke to her willpower that she'd resisted the temptation to give up and go back. She'd found a way to make the most of the fog and the difficulty. Were they preferable to a residue of anger against me?

"Fine. You're carrying a box of rooibosch tea, from South Africa. The box is red, blue, white, yellow. It's got an old-fashioned illustration of a mother handing a cup to her son at the kitchen table. You've stayed loyal to this brand. And though you don't like to admit it, you buy it in bags rather than as loose tea because you can't be bothered to brew a pot each time."

I did have the satisfaction of seeing her blush, beneath her tan. She said, "That's a good guess—"

"It wasn't a guess."

"—but I simply don't remember you." Her eyes warmed slightly. "I wish I did, because you seem to remember me."

"You must've noticed that most people here remember more than you. They know exactly who they used to be."

"They say they do, but who can tell? It might be their imagination." She bit her lip. "I've never felt full of memories. I know I must've been someone before I arrived, since everybody else was. I don't even know how old I was when I died. I remember feeling an utter blank before that Dutch woman called me Suzy."

At that moment, more than ever, I wanted to take her in my arms.

I said, "You were forty-three. A year younger than I. Except you always looked a decade younger, because you took such wonderful care of yourself. You supported us both when I stopped being able to play the piano. You took on too many students, you were teaching more than was healthy. You were even writing a book on taking control of one's body, before you got too ill to finish."

Though this was all new to her, and too much to absorb, it must've felt true. Maybe memory loss was softened by being dead. Since you were granted so much of the world here, so much past and future to wander through, amnesia might lessen the dangerous urge to give up, to go back. And if you didn't remember anybody, there wasn't the hurt of not finding them.

THE LAND OF LATER ON

She said, "I see you have a lot to tell me. But I can't hear more now. Maybe we can try a walk tomorrow, or the day after. Or next week. I might leave on a trip."

I couldn't hear this. "To Burma, I'll bet." Suppose she didn't come back?

"I've been already. Have you?"

"Nope." Thank you, sir, this completes the examination. The committee regret to inform you that you have squandered your only opportunity.

"Or," she said, "we could have lunch sometime. I find there's less pressure at lunch than dinner, don't you? For a first date, I mean."

We'd been through this before, summer 1987.

"Let's decide now," I said. "I don't have a way to get in touch with you. And there's no way for you to find me." I could feel her ready to walk off. "Please."

I hated the way I sounded—imploring and desperate. That tone of voice wouldn't have worked on the Lucy I knew. Probably not on this version, either.

She frowned. "If you insist."

"Why not tonight? I could meet you right here in front of Mistry's pharmacy, so you don't have to tell me where you live. Though I bet I know where you live."

That sure backfired. I saw alarm cross her face.

"No, not for the reason you think. Because you're living in our apartment. The one we shared for years. It was originally mine, then you moved in from your studio. It's only a couple of blocks from here. I bet there was a small piano when you arrived. If you haven't gotten rid of it, I'll play for you sometime."

At least my knowledge of that spinet struck a chord.

"I didn't get rid of it. And I know where I live." She stepped past me, and I made it clear I wasn't going to follow her. "All right, we can say seven."

"See you this evening, Lucy. By the way, I've got my playing back."

She read the loss in my eyes. She said evenly, "I'm sorry to disappoint you, Kip, but dinner is the best I can do."

LESSONS LEARNED

"I thought I might see you in a bad mood one of these days," said Whitman. He ushered me into Lucy's studio. "Settle down."

I'd taken a big chance looking for him in the past. Having watched Lucy stride off toward our apartment, the obvious plan was to sit tight all afternoon. If I risked shifting out of her present, there was the danger I'd never return precisely enough to find her. Yet if I didn't enlist Walt's help, I wouldn't know what to say to convince her, because I didn't understand what the hell was going on.

So I gritted my teeth, gambling I'd wind up on Duane Street soon after Walt returned from Tulsa. The day was bright, under a porcelain sky ready to shatter.

He was expecting me: the door swung in on my second agitated knock.

He sat me down, and made me explain everything. I stood up and paced a few times before sitting again. He rubbed his hands together as I spoke.

"Do you know a better word than *adhesiveness*?" he said. "That's what enabled you to find Lucy at the very moment in a yawning future when she stepped from Mistry's pharmacy. Five minutes in either direction, never mind five weeks or months or years, you'd have missed her. It's what enabled you to find me. Can anyone doubt adhesiveness as the greatest instinct in nature? Such moments allow us to see the world clearly, to perceive lines of force. To traverse dimensions. Yet the malevolent guidebook denies it! Pretends it doesn't exist, that we're all alone on a tumultuous sea, whirled ever farther from those who matter most! As if it must always be this way, there's no point in striving, and nothing any of us can do!"

I'd learned not to interrupt WW in high gear, it was best to let him run down. When he stopped I said, "I think Lucy believes me, though she sure doesn't trust me." I didn't bring up why. "But I know the way her mind works. Within a block she'll have come up with a dozen explanations for how I knew all I knew. She can't feel in her bones who she was. And no matter what I say, she won't remember me."

Whitman murmured, "I knew this would happen."

"What's that supposed to mean?"

"I haven't been completely forthcoming with you. Don't be angry."

Now what? How long had he known?

"I foresaw this," he said, "because I had already spoken with Lucy about who she thinks she used to be." He put up his hand. "Do give me a chance to explain, dear friend."

"So we could have found her at any moment?" *Dear friend?* "You knew where she was all along?"

He looked shocked. "Of course not. I would never lie to you that way."

"Tell me which way you would lie to me."

I watched him tamp down his forlorn was-ever-a-man-more-misunderstood expression. He said nervously, "I promise you, I had absolutely no idea, beyond those many diverse pamphlets, where she might be. Indeed, we only found her trail because of your insight. As it turns out, you found her yourself. Without my help."

You bastard.

"I suspected—and correct me if I'm wrong—that if I warned you Lucy was suffering from severe amnesia, you might not continue searching. I feared that you would lose heart, no matter what I or Billy said. One moment's hasty desperation, and you'd have decided to go back. Very reasonably."

"I'm not a reasonable person."

"We encounter this all the time. We've learned what sometimes works. And what never does."

We? Oh, right, his underground cabal. What else weren't they telling me?

"I hoped that if you found Lucy, and spoke with her, and came to learn of her affliction from her rather than from me, the outcome might be different. She might believe you, whereas she'd never believe me. You don't realize how common her situation is. Multitudes arrive in the afterlife lacking any strand of identity. With even less to go on than your Lucy. Without keys to unlock the necessary doors. Unscrew the locks from the doors, I say. I did warn you this sometimes happens." He paused. "It befell me once, most searingly, with someone I cared for."

He did not have to say what was suddenly evident: such amnesias weren't random strands of memory blindness, or bad luck. If Lucy didn't recall who I was to the point of erasing who *she* was, it meant that my wound had been deep; that no matter what she'd said before dying, she hadn't been able to forgive me. It wasn't the only time I'd chosen music over her, just the very last and the very worst. This was who I'd always been. Once here, she found it more comforting to forget herself than to remember us.

Four scattered years in the Land of Later On. They were my fault.

Had Walt done all he could for Lucy, once he deduced her identity? I doubted that. For him the truth meant elaboration; it wasn't his style to tell anything plain. I said, "Being welcomed by somebody who calls you the wrong name can't help."

Walt shook his head. "If you arrived here sure of yourself, it wouldn't make the slightest difference. Suppose your childhood doctor had called you Harold, or Frank? You'd have politely reminded him and left it at that."

Walt had originally pretended it was without significance that Dr. McMillan, not Lucy, first greeted me in the afterlife. He'd also pretended never to have known Lucy. That was the windiest lie of all.

It would get me nowhere to show my anger: I needed him.

"What's uncommon," he continued—as if he could talk me into letting him off the hook—"and most inspiring, are the enthusiasm and courage Lucy uses to face this every day. Most amnesiacs turn back. Notice how the guidebook shrills away at the cruel assumption that its readers know their pasts in detail. Can you imagine how grievous this is for those with no idea who they were?"

That damned guidebook again, his personal obsession. "I can imagine."

"Perhaps you appreciate, now, why I urged her to travel. To experience as much of the Land of Later On as she could. I sensed that she would be invigorated the more she saw. The longer she remained the more chance there was that you'd arrive. And find me, then her. Did I do the wrong thing? I don't believe I did."

A hearty, well-intentioned man, but clueless about normal human relations. Or else (I never decided which it was) a champion manipulator.

"When did you two have this conversation?"

He arched his eyebrows. "Oh, it must've been shortly after she died. I'd already moved in and—such is the sweet paradox of the afterlife—the place was as she left it. I'd resided for years. She knocked one morning, she could not have been nicer. Or more confused. Said she wasn't sure why she'd come, but had the most uncanny sensation she'd lived here once. Naturally, after she had a chance to gaze around at her belongings, she felt more at home."

"Except she believed her name was Suzy."

"Yes, but I could tell as soon as I opened the door that she was an amnesiac. They have a look about them, you know, something missing behind their eyes. Just as the ones who aren't long for this world take on a pallor before they go back; if you can read the telltales, you know before they do. Anyway, I told her I thought her name might be Lucy. You have to be delicate, you can't plop scrapbooks in front of them and say, *Look at all this, these were your family, this was your life.* It was tempting, but I didn't want to lose her." He saw my reaction. "Didn't want her to go back, I mean."

"Did you introduce yourself? Did she believe who *you* were?"

"Right away." He preened, a tad. "Happily, I had a speech to make at one of the important libraries that evening, so I was looking like my older self again. That national monument you've seen in the Brady portrait. The grim gray statue all the busy birds crap on." He gave a satisfied chuckle at his alliteration. "Not a bad one for a Monday. So she had no trouble recognizing me. You know her much better than I do, of course, but she struck me as someone for whom belief is kinesthetic. If her body tells her something's true, she believes it. If it doesn't, all the paperwork and fancy arguments in the world won't convince her."

Yes, that was my Lucy.

I said, "Maybe it would've been different if she'd stayed here a while. Surrounded by her possessions. If she hadn't left so quickly."

"She did stay. I offered to move out, since I don't mind changing premises, never have. I knew you'd turn up sooner or later, and it was a sure bet you'd search here. I'd learned from Billy, purely by chance, that you lived together uptown, and although she didn't have any recollection of the place, I felt she might one day."

"She's there now. Or three decades from now. Doesn't connect it with me."

"At that moment she would have none of it. Refused to recognize your photo, though she recognized her own handwriting on the back. She acknowledged that this studio was hers, but she wasn't about to evict Walt Whitman. It took my most eloquent powers of persuasion to get her to move in with her favorite poet, but it wasn't until I made myself young again that she let me sleep on the floor."

So he'd lived with her more recently than I had.

"It wouldn't be for long, she insisted, because she planned to keep moving. I decided that the best bet was to direct her journeyings. Fortunately, some of my cohorts are tactically quite experienced."

"Your phony travel agents."

That pained him. "I'll not pass along your characterization of their artistry. It took unique insight to glean from her bookshelves where she'd want to visit, then prepare enough pamphlets to keep her on an odyssey until you might appear. As it happened, your friend Billy recognized Lucy from my description. Even mentioned that she would never introduce him to her most flexible students. And he thought—I hope this won't disappoint you— you might be an ideal candidate for early death."

"Takes one to know one. His diet was suicidal. But he's smarter than he looks."

"Indeed, he wrote every one of those pamphlets, to captivate her. It was a pleasure to teach her how to travel and encourage her to linger in each historical locale. I escorted her to witness the unveiling of Haghia Sophia in Constantinople fifteen centuries ago, and if I say so myself, it was a poetic masterpiece to shift two people so far. The mendacious guidebook tells us that to go back such a distance is impossible, but if you know what you're doing. . . . "

Next he was going to sing about the tarnished moonlight on the Bosphorus.

I said, as calmly as I could, "How much duplicity should I serve her for dinner?"

I wondered how many disjointed couples he and his associates were trying to link up. At that moment I realized he looked a lot less shaggy than before. Combed and trimmed, post-Tulsa: a new Walt. He saw that I noticed.

"My twice-a-year haircut. Despite what I know to the contrary, I always feel mortality upon me when I lose things in groups." He added quietly, "Don't worry, I intend to accompany you to where Lucy's waiting. If you like, I'll join you the first few minutes at dinner. She won't expect us together, and that may go an estimable distance toward convincing her. I don't believe she caught sight of me on Nuku Hiva. I'm not lying when I say I haven't seen her in a long time. But she considers me a friend, and she trusts me. Not for who I was, the barnacled name, but what I did for her. I shall explain every step of the way, I'll take full responsibility, I'll vouch for you. Then I shall leave you two alone, and it will be up to you to recount as much as you see fit about who she was. My only advice is to proceed slowly, be judicious and gentle, and do not expect great things."

"I don't even expect her to be there."

He said, "I'm a little worried, Kip. You look pale."

III

SEND-OFF

THE RETURN

At least there were no complications when Walt shifted us to the evening's appointment with Lucy. We were early; it was 6:40, according to a clock outside Mistry's. Plenty of sunlight.

"She's upstairs in our apartment, having second thoughts," I muttered.

He grasped me by the elbow. "Let's call on her there."

"Are you crazy? She's suspicious as it is. I accosted her on the street."

"What I love most about love," said Whitman, "is the way it perpetually reminds us how much is in the eye of the beholder. You can't possibly realize what your certainty will have meant to her. You are the sole window on her lost identity. She has gotten along without it for ages, for many meandering miles, so she is understandably reluctant to embrace it or you blindly. Yet she has kept hoping this day would come. I promise she will not stand up the boyfriend she won't let herself remember. Nor feel threatened if we call on her together. If I say so myself, seeing you alongside me will be the gesture of approval she needs. Come along."

Now that I was only a couple of blocks and a quarter hour away, I found myself trying to put it off. I was still formulating what to say—that I knew why she hadn't been able to admit who she was. Taking the blame might not do any good.

Walt didn't let my arm go until we stood before my brown-stone.

"Suppose she won't buzz us in? There's a futuristic security system."

"I have smashed through many a wall in my time. Up those stairs, please."

In the entryway he said, "Which apartment? Ah, yes, the one with no name." He buzzed emphatically, then buzzed again when there was no immediate response.

"You're not shy, are you."

"Never got me anyplace," said Whitman. "Consult my many biographies, and despair." Lucy's voice came through the intercom. "Mr. Walt Whitman, at your service!" he barked, and the newfangled glass doors parted for us.

"You see? Be restrained in war, but in love be bold." Leading me up to the second floor, he said conversationally, "Jazz on the left, dirty books on the right. I don't suppose you've said hello to our friend Boyd's nephew."

Oddly, I felt winded. "He was a twit. Embarrassed by Billy."

"One must be forgiving. Pornography isn't for everybody. By the way, I'm sorry to report that Billy seems to have gone missing."

"He's probably researching 17th century harems."

"I wish it were so. Ah, here we are."

He knocked confidently on my old door. Both locks had been replaced by hand slots. So much for a trusting future.

The door swung open and there she was, as stunning as I remembered, in a slim gray dress we'd found in Paris and a braided necklace in white gold I'd bought her to celebrate ten years together. Surely she was wearing them for me.

"Walt, this is a surprise—" she began, then caught sight of his accomplice. "Yes, a big surprise."

"I think you know my friend Kip," said Whitman. "Your friend Kip."

"He didn't mention that you were friends."

"An oversight, no doubt. It astonishes me how very many people I have known over the centuries. Fortunately I maintain a remarkable memory for names and faces, so I rarely find myself being downright rude." He was blathering, trying to relax her with talk—a waste of time. Her eyes were on me, anyhow, not him.

I said quietly, "It was Walt's idea to come here first and vouch for me."

Face to face, I was worried that my guide wouldn't want to leave us.

"You know," said Whitman, "I've never visited this apartment. I've heard so much about it, and I can't tell you how many enjoyable evenings I've spent across the hall, yarning with your former neighbor about the tribulations of publishing. He spoke so highly about the decades living beside the two of you."

"I don't know who you mean," said Lucy.

"Fellow named Billy Boyd." Walt glanced at me; clearly the name didn't ring a bell. "He often spoke of how very happy you and Kip were."

Weirdly, I couldn't seem to catch my breath. Nor could I speak. All our conversations these last years— that I'd created in my mind, and coveted—fled.

"Never met him. I guess you two should come in for a minute." Perhaps she too was worried Walt might stick around. "You're loyal to rooibosch, aren't you?" This last to me as we entered.

"More than ever. You look wonderful, Lucy."

"You don't look so great." She peered at me curiously as she shut the door behind us. "Do you feel all right?"

"Maybe a little woozy," I admitted.

"Better rest," said Whitman. He took one arm and led me, past the little piano missing an octave at each end, toward a white sofa I'd never seen before. But I had a quick inspiration, pulled out the stool of my faithful spinet, and sat down.

"Lucy, this is how we met. I was playing Chopin in a bank. You came in to make a deposit." I was already a few measures in to the *Prelude in E Minor*. "I was playing this when you spoke to me. We'd been staring at each other for weeks."

The piano made it feasible for me to speak. I got my breath back.

"Doesn't sound very polite, to interrupt you."

She was watching my hands, but there wasn't the slightest spark of recognition in her eyes. I heard Whitman rustle impatiently behind us. Couldn't he take a hint?

"I recognize that piece, of course," she said. "But the rest of it—I'm sorry, I can't pretend. Are you sure it was me?"

"Of course I'm sure."

"A lot of people look alike."

"They absolutely do not," said Walt, "if you offer them your full attention."

She might argue with me, but not with Walt Whitman.

"For heaven's sake," he went on, "do not be ruled by your amnesia. There is more to who you are, I swear to you, than an unfortunate forgetfulness."

"You keep telling me to remember. It's like asking me to move a missing limb. It's not there anymore."

Missing limb? I knew all about that sensation—this was not going remotely the way I intended. I felt waves that I could vanish at any instant, then they'd pass. At least Chopin, useless Chopin, was finally over with.

"When I was done at the bank," I said, "we went out for lunch together. But first you played something for me." I let the prelude's last sonority die, then ripped into Chopin's *Minute Waltz* as if there were no tomorrow. Nothing wrong with *my* memory, though I hadn't gone through the piece in years.

She took a breath. "You think I played that for you?"

"I know you did. Beautifully."

"I could never have attempted that piece. I'm sorry, you've got me confused with another woman."

"I promise you I don't. Look, let me try something else." My words were just noise; no matter what I said I wasn't going to talk her into believing any of it. In desperation I went into that haunted Jobim bossa, *How Insensitive*, playing for her as if in apology. Sixteen bars in, halfway through, I felt her stiffen alongside me. I'm sorry, Lucy, if you don't like what you're hearing, this is who I am, this is all I have left to offer you.

Then she put her hands tenderly, familiarly, on my upper back. "Your shoulders always flex like this when you play. I don't know if that's what I'm supposed to say, but it's what I remember."

"Aha," said Whitman.

Was I going to topple, in front of the piano? I was not. Her touch, her calm, were holding me up.

"Thank you for looking so hard for me, Kip," she said softly.

I tried to say *Welcome back* but abruptly felt I might faint. Years of frustration, years of loneliness. I managed to get haltingly through the melody, my right fingers starting to close up, before I let both hands drop. Instantly Lucy and Walt were on either side, hauling me over to the sofa. I sat back heavily, seized by the electrified twinges whose attacks on my right leg had become so familiar in the prior world. There was no way my disease could strike in the afterlife, was there? Maybe it was nervousness at being with Lucy. I closed my eyes, imagining a horrible alternate present in which we'd met in front of Mistry's—by now we'd be at some restaurant, the cattle prod on my leg. Without the music's blessing it would all have gone wrong.

"You look terrible," she said, with a voice that was suddenly beginning to know me. "I'll get that tea under way."

"Forget the tea," Whitman ordered. His tone was so stern, so unlike his usual manner, that against my will I opened my eyes. He was standing in front of me and speaking slowly, as if to make sure that despite the fact I was underwater I would hear every syllable. "Pay attention, please. While you and I were in the Marquesas, our friend Billy disappeared. This would not ordinarily be worth noticing, except he left me and my colleagues a note. He went back."

I said, "I don't believe you." God Almighty, what was happening? My leg was being drained of normalcy, as if somebody were vacuuming away my strength. Lucy sat down beside me and handed me a glass of water; automatically I reached across my body to take it with my left hand, once again my only good hand.

"We were all very surprised. We'd discussed this many times. Our idea was that somebody might return with an accurate memory of what it's like here. Bearing a detailed account. If he or she became a writer the story would be published one day, even if it were ultimately read not as a trustworthy memoir, but as fiction."

The water temporarily revived me. "Billy would never be so gullible. He thought anybody who went back was a chump."

Lucy got up to refill my glass. She couldn't conceal the fear on her face.

"You've known him longer than I," said Walt. "Nevertheless, I have always sensed a futile heroic act in his soul, waiting to be released. And there's not a sign of him, except for his note. Had the plan been successful, he'd have put out the account we all spoke of writing, that he must have prepared, and come back to tell the tale. As someone else, no doubt. But he hasn't, I'm afraid."

"Come back how?" said Lucy.

It was glory to feel her body next to mine again, to reach over and take that glass from her hand again, gulp the water as if I could taste her in every swallow.

"Suicide," said Whitman.

A chill went through me. "He's gorging on cheeseburgers somewhere," I managed, though I didn't believe it. "Why are you telling me this?"

"Because you're about to go back. I can see it in your face."

"No fucking way."

"Spoken like a true New Yorker. I wish it weren't so."

"You told me a person has to want to."

Insects were crawling all over my skin, no use pretending they weren't. It was much worse dying the second time.

"I told you," said Walt, "people acquire a pallor. I got a bit suspicious in Simla, and I've kept a careful eye on you. It's happening to you right now. It seems you weren't as successful as we thought when you committed suicide. A neighbor was able to revive you."

"I've been dead for weeks!"

"Time is different here, I warned you." He frowned. "I can't lie, Kip. I've known about this. Somebody from years later told me the story. I didn't want to alarm you. Don't worry, you'll go back as you. We have to try everything to send you back fully intact. With luck we'll see you here again one day. Lucy, help me walk him into the bedroom. That's where you killed yourself originally, isn't it?"

Holding my arms, they got me standing. It took all the determination I could muster not to collapse. They didn't expect me to think fast, and before they could stop me I sat triumphantly back down on the sofa. As long as I stayed there, I was safe.

"Get up," Whitman commanded. Lucy looked horrified. Not that I could blame her—this wasn't turning out much of a date.

"I can't."

"We're going to do this until we get you onto that bed."

"It's too far."

Impossible to convey to the uninitiated how much force is needed to make several steps across a room. The one advantage of this disease, a real estate effect nobody mentions, is that as time goes on all your rooms get larger.

"Ever want to see Lucy again?" Stupid question. "Do as I say."

When you put it like that—

It seemed to take forever, but they got me across the kitchen to our darkened bedroom. I sprawled gratefully; the pillow smelled of Lucy. Walt, merciful to the end, rolled me on my back so I could gaze up at them both. My right wrist began to twitch, as it used to on bad days, but there was a new sensation of someone shoving against my chest.

Stop that, I said aloud—or thought, because I didn't hear my own words. *Will you please stop that?*

Lucy was sitting on the bed. She switched on our bedside lamp to see me better, and I saw her blink and frown. No wonder, I was pouring sweat.

She said, "I remember being in this room with you. I remember trying to hold on to your arm, I was so worried. But I think I was the one lying here."

One of her hands touched my face, just as I'd always imagined feeling at the moment I died, because once my disease hit I never expected to outlive her. Instead it'd been my hand stroking *her* forehead at the exact moment she went. You flatter yourself that you fear the worst, then life shows no mercy and proves you wrong.

My one good hand joined up with her other hand. Incredible, that twined fingers can mean so much.

She said, "I was so frightened that you'd be left for years without me—"

"Listen to me, Kip," said Whitman. "I need you to do me a favor."

Impeccable timing. *Don't interrupt her.* Once again I couldn't speak.

"I want you to take something back with you." He folded the malleable fingers of my unresponsive hand around a book. He pressed hard, and for an instant's shock, I felt his powerful being flow into my motionless claw. "You know what this is. Hang on tight. Bring it back with you if you can, so you can speak truth to its lies, page after page, before you rejoin us."

At least, pressing it into my weakened hand, he knew that smuggling the guidebook didn't matter as much as Lucy's clasp on the hand that was still alert. He was staring directly into my eyes. It took all my will to turn my head so my last sight would be of her.

"He's going now," she said to Walt. "I can feel him going."

It would've been much easier if the person gripping my shoulders stopped shaking me, back and forth, like a terrier shakes a squeaky toy in its jaws. I took a breath and closed my eyes.

"Stay with me, my darling," Lucy said from a surprising distance, though I felt her hand on my face. "Stay with me, Kip."

Once again a pause, a swath of infinite blackness across my consciousness, and I was through to the other side in one enormous exhalation. Some jackass was jerking me violently about, attempting to wake me when it was killingly obvious that all I needed to do, all I wanted out of life this hot July afternoon, was to be allowed to rest. Why is it so difficult to be left in peace?

"Stay with me," said the brute, heaving me up and down. "Stay with me, Kip."

I recognized his voice. The words were Lucy's, but that crude register could only belong to Billy Boyd's son of a bitch nephew. He slapped me a couple of times—amazing how people grab whatever pitiful opportunities come their way, to prove a point—and when that didn't work, he got up. Thankfully he scurried into the other room and left me alone so I could go back to sleep. I heard him lift the phone, dial three numbers, and urgently provide my address along with a melodramatic speech about walking in to "borrow" some ice, finding an empty bottle of sleeping pills beside me, etc. If you're going to commit suicide, take it from an expert: on no account forget to lock your door. Otherwise you're utterly defenseless against a Nosy Parker (to borrow Lucy's expression).

I did my best to drop off to generous oblivion once more, but my savior came back and started slapping me again. "Don't worry," he said, "we'll have your stomach pumped in no time."

The buzzer sounded from downstairs, and this ultra-clean Boyd leaped up to welcome the health squad. In the ensuing *tramp-tramp-tramp* I awoke enough to shove the guidebook—which had survived, but stank to high heaven—under the edge of the sweaty sheets, where no one would spot it.

Before they lifted me like any would-be corpse onto a stretcher, without the slightest notion of the journey I'd returned from, I did notice that my pillow no longer smelled of Lucy. Only me.

EMBRACING THE INEVITABLE

The watchword of a guidebook must be its dedication to truth. The reader is cautioned that the Land of Later On depends on a healthily revolving population. No portrait should be deemed final; a guide can provide only the latest information until the next version comes along.

The Editor welcomes any suggestions helpful visitors may offer, though no two experiences of this bourne are alike. Before contradicting these pages, the newcomer ought to be aware that the guidebook is based on unmatched research. Its success may be measured by the enlightenment a visitor derives from his brief stay, no matter how intense and unforeseen its frustrations. The afterlife is, quite simply, not for everybody.

If the traveler has been able to dispose of his limited time to advantage, then the Editor's tireless efforts shall have been sufficiently rewarded.

Lies, lies, nothing but lies.

At first I was bewildered to be back—although three days in a hospital ward for the unstable and hence untrustworthy, sharing a room divided by a curtain with an elderly man who woke alternately sobbing or screaming, whom no one visited and who kept his TV going even when asleep, did tug me toward a semblance of reality. Small mercies: I wasn't strapped down, like he was.

It didn't take long for me to decide I must've imagined it all, though a part of me knew I had not. The sole proof, I told myself, would be if the guidebook were waiting in my sheets. Even if it had disintegrated from contact with the stale air in this land of the living, if any of its stench remained that would be evidence enough.

One morning I put on the clothes I'd died in, waved good-bye to my comatose roommate, and wobbled down the hall to shake hands with the nurses who'd kept me from garrotting myself on their watch. I confirmed with the psych on duty that I'd learned the error of my ways, deserved to be discharged, and would see him next week, then rode the elevator. This condemned man had breakfasted heartily, and the hospital thoughtfully provided me with a new cane. I was anxious to grab a taxi and find out if the guidebook was waiting in my bed. If so, it would only take me a half hour to pull myself downstairs, lurch over to Third Avenue, and buy another bottle of sleeping pills from the reliable Mistry. This time I'd lock my apartment door. By lunchtime I'd be back in the Land of Later On with Lucy.

And if the book wasn't there, after those pills I'd still be infinitely better off.

You're probably expecting me to say that, much to my horror, I tore off the sheets with the limited strength left me by my disease and realized that there was no guide, it had all been a dream. I crumpled to the floor, my hopes shattered and my fears vindicated, overpowered by grief and madness.

In fact, no. A corner of the guidebook peeped from the edge of the sheets; I pulled it out and held it to my face. It no longer stank, and as I flipped with relief through its pages of informative and misleading print, all I'd just left sprang out at me, every conversation with Dr. McMillan and Billy and Walt, every inch of my odyssey, every minute with Lucy. You'll think me a weakling, but I sat down on the edge of the bed and cried. When I wiped my face, I found I was laughing.

I got myself into the other room, ignored the piano I could now no longer play, and settled myself onto the worn sofa to do a little sentimental reading. Late morning sun streamed through the two windows. Perhaps it would be a worthwhile experiment to try carrying the book in the other direction. For all I knew, I was the only person who'd succeeded in bringing back an artifact from the afterlife—what would Walt say if I managed to return him the guide in one piece?

I may not have been thinking straight at this slope of the morning, but I could hear his invective. He hadn't wrapped my fingers around the book to find out what, scientifically, would happen; he had, as usual, vaster things on his mind.

Well, he'd chosen the wrong messenger. If he'd been forthcoming from the start, had his cabal done less talking and more typing, he'd have handed me not the guidebook but a meticulous assault on its message, written by the finest minds the afterlife could offer. They'd had all the time they needed to scribble their tract over and over until they got it absolutely right, every syllable, every argument. I'd have brought *that* back with me, to circulate worldwide. They might call themselves an underground movement, and Billy might've sacrificed his existence on their behalf, but if you asked me, they were amateurs with no idea what they were doing.

I turned the guide's pages disbelievingly, read one lie after another with a fresh perspective, darted from each cunning chapter to the next, carried on that conversation with myself, laid the blame squarely on Whitman's shoulders. And, as he planned, wound up asking myself what Lucy would say if I explained that, yes, the guidebook survived the journey, but once here—even knowing I could rejoin her in the Land of Later On whenever I liked and she'd be waiting, no amnesia anymore—I backed out of the task I was entrusted with. Backed out of a chance to do something useful for a change, that might benefit countless people if I did it well.

So what? Other suicides, rescued by some busybody, must've come back like me with memories of the Land of Later On. Or maybe not. Maybe without the guidebook as a talisman to reawaken it in detail, they'd convince themselves it was a posthumous hallucination. Doomed to fade.

Yet the quandary of Billy Boyd, Pornographer, Esq., kept nagging away. I had the sharp instinct that Walt again hadn't been entirely truthful. Why would Billy return? Even on his most charitable days he wasn't a hero. If Walt knew, then Billy also knew he couldn't prevent his jerk nephew from saving me. But he never put much faith in people's abilities to do something they weren't cut out for—he'd insisted on editing the liner notes to my CDs. Perhaps Billy had decided, in some illogical moment, that although *he* hadn't been a suicide, if he returned with his own treatise gripped in both unwashed paws, he might read it years from now, remind himself who he'd once been, and publish the damning book I'd never write.

That was it. He'd come back so I wouldn't have to attempt writing this, certain it was beyond me. And failed miserably: he'd never brought with him and successfully published that treatise, since Walt would've learned about it from the future. Nor had he identifiably reappeared in the Land of Later On. Poor chump.

I found myself snarling as these prospects ricocheted violently in my head. I struggled downstairs and over to Third Avenue to secure those pills, brought them upstairs—the guidebook was still there, accusing me from the sofa—and I made the mistake of sitting down beside it to take a nap and sleep on the decision. Nap? I could've worried the bottle open and chased down the full lethal dose with a few glasses of cold water. If I had, believe me, we wouldn't be enjoying this conversation.

When I awakened I ate the organic turkey sandwich prepared by Mistry's chubby wife which I'd chosen to offset any suspicion about the pills, since I'd bought a similar bottle a few days earlier. I glanced through a few more chapters, reflected a bit on what Walt hoped I would do, remembered how familiar Lucy's hands had felt. The guidebook wouldn't go away.

So, six sweaty weeks later, here we are.

FAMOUS LAST WORDS

One secret Walt didn't impart, because I had to leave suddenly, was how you convince people of what they don't want to hear. He was a master at this; maybe it helped that he was able to speak aloud the secrets many were already saying quietly to themselves, within the solitude of their own skulls. I, on the other hand, didn't have the slightest idea how to go about the persuasion this book seemed to call for.

Over the course of writing I became surprisingly attached to it, far more than I expected since it was begun for the wrong reasons. Perhaps I was misled by the labor, for my disease was toughening rapidly; some days it was all I could do to put in an hour of dictating. Or perhaps because it turned out to be about my love for Lucy, and not the anti-guidebook I set out to write. Nevertheless I was under no illusions that the world was howling for a memoir of the afterlife. I certainly wasn't going to postpone suicide until a publisher turned up. My plan was to offer my manuscript along with photocopies of the incriminating passages I quoted. And if they needed to see the actual guidebook? Okay, I'd leave it for the authorities to stumble on when the stench of my body got bad enough.

The closer I've gotten to the end, though, the more nervous I've grown about not being believed. But who would bother making this stuff up? Why should I care if it never sees the light of day? I'll have kept my bargain to Billy, to Walt, to Lucy. Once it leaves my hands, I'm free to go.

The farther along I got, too, the more convinced I became that there was little in what I had to say that would strike people as good news. To me it was *all* good news, the deal of a lifetime. Yet nobody likes the suggestion that virtually everything they've thought is wrong.

Then yesterday, hours after I finished, I was nagged by worry that I might've overlooked some more pungent excerpts from the guidebook. To verify my choices I pulled open the dresser drawer where I've kept the thing in a manila envelope. I shouldn't have been surprised; it was smarter than I. The envelope remained, but inside were only spoonfuls of paper dust, and tiny flakes of the red leatherette cover to taunt me. The old-fashioned guide had contained an up-to-date self-destruct mechanism, and because I was never sure which pages I'd ultimately quote, I hadn't photocopied any. My only proof, alas, lay in my own words.

I had no maps, no photographs to offer a publisher. Just a pile of pages. And now that I've about reached the end, I doubt I have many illusions left. Well, as my trumpet mentor used to say, that's show biz.

So, you ask, is that all there is? Having come this far with me, naturally you feel you deserve to know the whole truth and nothing but the truth. Since I don't know you and you barely know me, how can we trust each other? This book is a lot to swallow, I'm sure.

As I said at the beginning, I don't expect to be believed, and I don't expect to be understood. You can offer people as much happiness and beauty as you like, this was my profession for years, but they have to be in the mood; and the same holds true for a sense of self-worth which lasts. That's the gigantic question the Land of Later On sets before everyone. The afterlife guarantees you all anybody might want except the right person to share it with, so the problem becomes one of your own sufficiency. Good luck with that, when your time comes.

I've done my best to write with enthusiasm about the power of adhesiveness—Whitman's word for friendship even between strangers, and these days the word I prefer for art. From boyhood I had immortal longings, yet the fact remains that despite my best nights I was nothing more than a first-rate saloon piano player. Which sounds like plenty at this late date. The musician I became will be totally forgotten once all my former colleagues vanish, and the great maw of posterity will snore on, as if I'd never dared disturb its sleep. Who cares? The gigs are better in the afterlife, the pianos perfectly in tune, listeners pay attention, and nobody waters the drinks.

Put your trust in adhesiveness, I hear Walt saying. As a musician, I always did: the capacity of people to speak intimately to each other, to listen and understand completely. Nothing else matters. Since you're reading this, it means first that Walt's vague plan for publication succeeded, and second (the best news of all, I promise), that I've flown the coop and am no longer here.

I'll tell you where I am, at this very moment: exactly where I'm meant to be, swimming through night alongside Lucy in our shared private ocean. Not worried about who we were but only alive to who we are, like two blind fish who can find their path in darkened depths so long as we remain together. Think of me that way.

Undoubtedly about now a small voice in each of you must be asking how much of this you should believe, and whether it's what it says it is—a useful account of a journey that you in turn will eventually make—or, instead, a work written by a man contemplating suicide for self-evident reasons. Almost ready to do the deed, imagining in hopeful despair and occasional wonder what might lie ahead.

You'll know soon enough.